Unlikely
SWEETHEARTS

AN AMISH CHRISTMAS STORY

JENNIFER
SPREDEMANN

Published in Indiana by *Blessed Publishing*.
www.jenniferspredemann.com

All Scripture quotations are taken from the *King James Version* of the *Holy Bible*.

Cover design by *iCreate Designs* ©
Formatting by *Polgarus Studio*

ISBN: 978-1-940492-55-1
10 9 8 7 6 5 4 3 2 1

Get a FREE short story as my thank you gift when you sign up for my newsletter here: www.jenniferspredemann.com

BOOKS by JENNIFER SPREDEMANN

Learning to Love – Saul's Story (Sequel to Chloe's Revelation)

AMISH BY ACCIDENT TRILOGY
Amish by Accident
*Englisch on Purpose (*Prequel to *Amish by Accident)*
*Christmas in Paradise (*Sequel to *Amish by Accident*)
(co-authored with Brandi Gabriel)

AMISH SECRETS SERIES
An Unforgivable Secret - Amish Secrets 1
A Secret Encounter - Amish Secrets 2
A Secret of the Heart - Amish Secrets 3
An Undeniable Secret - Amish Secrets 4
A Secret Sacrifice - Amish Secrets 5 (co-authored
with Brandi Gabriel)
A Secret of the Soul - Amish Secrets 6
A Secret Christmas – Amish Secrets 2.5 (co-authored
with Brandi Gabriel)

AMISH BIBLE ROMANCES
An Amish Reward (Isaac)
An Amish Deception (Jacob)
An Amish Honor (Joseph)
An Amish Blessing (Ruth)
An Amish Betrayal (David)

AMISH COUNTRY BRIDES

The Trespasser (Amish Country Brides)
The Heartbreaker (Amish Country Brides)
The Charmer (Amish Country Brides)
The Drifter (Amish Country Brides)

NOVELETTES

Cindy's Story – An Amish Fairly Tale Novelette 1
Rosabelle's Story – An Amish Fairly Tale Novelette 2

CHRISTMAS

Unlikely Santa
Unlikely Sweethearts

OTHER

Love Impossible

COMING 2020 (Lord Willing)

An Unexpected Christmas Gift (Amish Christmas Miracles Collection)
The Giver (Amish Country Brides)

BOOKS by J.E.B. SPREDEMANN

Unofficial Glossary
of Pennsylvania Dutch Words

Ach – Oh

Bann – Shunning

Boppli/Bopplin – Baby/Babies

Bruder/Brieder – Brother/Brothers

Daed/Dat – Dad

Dawdi – Grandpa

Denki – Thanks

Der Herr – The Lord

Englischer – A non-Amish person

Fraa – Wife

G'may – Members of an Amish fellowship

Gott – God

Grossdawdi – Grandfather

Grossmammi – Grandmother

Gut – Good

Jah – Yes

Kinner – Children

Kumm – Come

Mamm – Mom

Mammi – Grandma

Ordnung – Rules of the Amish community

Rumspringa – Running around period for Amish youth

Wunderbaar – Wonderful

Youngie – a Youth

Author's Note

The Amish/Mennonite people and their communities differ one from another. There are, in fact, no two Amish communities exactly alike. It is this premise on which this book is written. I have taken cautious steps to assure the authenticity of Amish practices and customs. Old Order Amish and New Order Amish may be portrayed in this work of fiction and may differ from some communities. Although the book may be set in a certain locality, the practices featured in the book may not necessarily reflect that particular district's beliefs or culture. This book is purely fictional and built around a fictional community, even though you may see similarities to real-life people, practices, and occurrences.

We, as *Englischers*, can learn a lot from the Plain People and their simple way of life. Their hard work, close-knit family life, and concern for others are to be applauded. As the Lord wills, may this special culture continue to be respected and remain so for many centuries to come, and may the light of God's salvation reach their hearts.

To my Lord and Saviour, Jesus Christ,
May the words of my mouth, the meditation of my
heart, and works of my hands bring You glory.

ONE

Wesley Stoltz knocked the snow off his work boots, then stepped into the comfy cabin he'd built for his bride two years prior. He blew warmth into his hands and rubbed them together. Winter had made its arrival early this year, but he didn't mind it one bit.

He briefly wondered how his Amish grandparents were faring in this weather. He couldn't imagine driving in this frigid air with only hot bricks and blankets to keep his family warm. Since his father's family had been from a very conservative Amish district, they'd only used open buggies—even in the dead of winter. Fortunately, Wesley had grown up *Englisch*. It was times like this he was most thankful for that fact.

"Cold out there?" Shannon, his beautiful wife, moved near and helped him out of his heavy coat.

"Mm…" He leaned down and planted a kiss on her

irresistible pink lips. "First things first—" he grinned "—and yes, I can't remember ever having a winter this cold. We must have a foot of snow out there."

"The kids will love it. I bet the pond is frozen over."

"Yes, but no one is to go out there until I test it."

An annoying buzz sounded from the refrigerator door. The kitchen timer.

Shannon swirled around and rushed to the oven, leaving Wesley bereft of the kisses he still anticipated. But delight quickly filled his senses as he inhaled the heady aroma of the apple pies she'd removed and set on top of the stove.

He moved close again and lightly yanked on her apron strings, thus pulling her into his embrace. "Have I ever told you how much I love you?"

Her eyes danced with something he couldn't put his finger on. "Once or twice." She moved to step away but he forbid it.

"Un-uh. Oh, no. You're not getting away that easy." His finger traced the shape of her lovely face, then gently tilted her chin up. When he recognized the reciprocating desire in his wife's eyes, he leaned down to claim the kiss he'd been anticipating since he'd left the house this morning.

"Are you guys kissing *again*?" Jaycee's complaint ruined the moment.

Lips still touching, they both laughed. Private moments in a houseful of children were few and far between.

"Jaycee, you're not supposed to interrupt when Wesley and I are busy." Shannon's hand flew to her hip and she looked pointedly at her seven-year-old brother. "What do you need?"

"You said we can ask Wesley about ice skating when he comes home. And I heard the timer go off. And I smelled dessert. And the baby's awake."

Shannon gestured to Wesley. "He's here. Ask away."

"Wesley, can we *pleeeaase* go ice skating on the pond?"

Wesley's frown met Jaycee's eager expression. "Absolutely not. We don't know if it's safe yet."

"But you said when it's frozen—"

"It has to be secure. You wait until I check it, okay? I don't want *any* of you going out there until I say it's safe. Got it?"

Jaycee's brow puckered. "Not even Bright?"

Wesley shook his head. "Not even Brighton. Got it?"

"Yeah, I got it," Jaycee mumbled.

"Jaycee." Wesley paused and crouched down to Jaycee's level. "Look at me."

He waited until Jaycee looked him in the eye.

"I'm not trying to ruin your fun. It can be *very* dangerous if we go out there before the ice is completely frozen. And just because it's frozen on top doesn't mean that it's safe. Promise me you'll stay away."

"I promise."

Wesley caught the disappointment in his young brother-in-law's voice. He understood the feeling. "I'll tell you what. If I go out there to check it and it isn't strong enough yet, how about if we go to the ice skating rink in Lawrenceburg?"

"For reals, Wesley?"

"Yes, for reals." He glanced up and winked at his wife. "That is, if your sister says it's okay."

"Can we, Shan? Can we? Pleeeeaaase?"

"*May* we." She shook her head. It seemed like trying to teach the children proper English was a never-ending task for his wife.

"May we? Pleeeeeaaase?"

She laughed. Saying no to Jaycee was always difficult. She glanced at Wesley. "When?"

"Oh, I don't know. This weekend, maybe?" He pulled out his cell phone. "I believe they're open until eight or nine, so we wouldn't be out too late."

"*Please*, Shan!"

"Jaycee, just let me think a minute," Shannon placed a hand on her forehead.

Concern rose as prickles on Wesley's neck. "You all right, babe?"

"Yeah, I'm fine. There's just a lot going on right now."

"Why don't you take a break from all of this? You've been working on Christmas preparations non-stop since December hit."

"You're exaggerating."

"Still. Go skating with us." He reached for her hand and brought her close. "It'll be a nice little date," he murmured in her ear.

A laugh exploded from her lips. "A nice date? With all the kids?"

"No, not all. I'm sure my parents or maybe Grandma and Grandpa would love to watch the youngest two."

"Yeah, okay. That sounds like fun," she acquiesced.

"Maybe we can invite Randy to come along. Mom said something about him bringing a 'significant other' home with him." Wesley couldn't picture his little brother with a steady girlfriend.

Shannon's brow arched. "Significant other? How significant?"

"We shall see."

"I can't see your brother settling down."

"I know, right? He's teased me relentlessly about being an old married man." Wesley shook his head, laughing.

"You're twenty-five, babe. Nowhere even close to old married man status."

"So you're okay with them coming along?"

"Sure, why not?"

"Okay then, I'll arrange everything." He stepped into the living room, heading toward the children's rooms to check on the other children. Just as soon as he finished greeting Brighton, Melanie, and Olivia, their one-year-old daughter, he reached for his cell phone to call his brother.

Randy whipped out his cell phone the moment it began vibrating in his pocket. He glanced down at the caller ID and answered. "What's up, Wes?"

"We're thinking of going ice skating this weekend. Would you and…"

"Lisa."

"Yeah, would you and Lisa like to join us?"

"Who's us?"

"Me, Shannon, Brighton, and Jaycee."

"Yeah, sure. We don't have any concrete plans yet. That sounds like fun. Just text me the details."

"Will do."

He clicked off his phone just as Lisa came into the room. "What sounds like fun?" She beamed.

"Ice skating this weekend." He raised his eyebrows twice in quick succession.

Lisa frowned. "Ice skating?" Had he heard disappointment in her voice?

"Yeah. Is something wrong?"

"I hate ice skating." She pouted.

"You do?" His brow arched, and his excitement plummeted.

She nodded.

"Oh. I already told Wesley—"

"Don't let me stop you from having fun."

"Well, what about you? What will you do?"

"I can just hang out here and read." She held up her cell phone. "Or catch up with my friends on social media."

"If you want to go along, there's a little room where you can chill while we're skating. And there's a fire outside. That way you won't miss out on coffee or hot cocoa afterwards."

"Sure. We can do that."

"Are you certain you're okay with it? Because I can just tell Wesley—"

"It's fine, Randy. Don't worry about me. I'm easy to please."

He smiled, remembering why he liked Lisa in the first place. She was definitely what he would call low maintenance. "Great."

TWO

Randy glided across the ice, enjoying the feel of the breeze cooling his face. He spun around, then glanced backward as he skated with ease, backside first. Lisa was really missing out. It was a shame she didn't enjoy ice skating. He hoped it wasn't something he'd have to give up if they ever considered a permanent relationship. Not that it was more important than the love of a woman. It was just that he and his brother Wesley had practically been on the ice since they'd been able to walk. It was one of his favorite winter pastimes.

He spun around again…just in time to knock a young woman off her feet.

"Oh, no!" He screeched to a full stop and reached for her hand to help her up. As their gazes met, he realized she looked familiar. "I'm so sorry. I…you were in my blind spot. I should have been watching where I was going better."

Ah, he'd never done that before—at least, not unintentionally. Wesley had been the recipient of many purposeful jabs and pushes as the brothers scuffled on the ice in times past. Mom had always worried one of them would break something. They hadn't, which she attributed to the spinach she'd coaxed them to eat growing up.

"No, it was me. I saw you coming but I couldn't get out of the way fast enough." The pretty brunette wiped her gloved hands on her jacket.

"I feel like I know you from somewhere. Have we met before?"

"You're Randy Stoltz. Wesley's brother, right?"

"Right." Recognition slowly began to dawn on him.

"I'm Holly. Holly Remington. I go to church with your parents. And your brother's family too." She glanced around. "In fact, I'm here with our singles group."

He slapped his forehead. Of course. Hadn't she and Wesley dated a few times? "Wait. Holly? Didn't you and my brother go out?"

Her cheeks flushed as she glanced toward where Wesley and Shannon skated hand-in-hand. "Uh, yeah."

He nodded, then stuck out his hand to greet her. "Randy."

"Yeah, I..." she left off laughing.

"Just ignore that last..." Was his face on fire?

Because it sure felt like it. "Yeah, you already…" He chuckled. "I'm sorry, I'm—"

"No, you're fine."

Her smile took a bit of the edge off his embarrassment. She had an incredible smile. Why hadn't he noticed it before?

Time to change the subject. "Look, I feel really bad about knocking you over. I guess I'm a real knockout, huh?" Oh, man, that was bad. Why was he being such an idiot tonight?

But she actually laughed at his corny joke. Lisa would have just rolled her eyes.

"Can I…may I buy you a hot cocoa?" He recovered.

"Oh." Her eyes widened and she looked behind him. "Are you here *alone*?"

"Ah, uh, no actually. I brought a date. She's hanging out in the little room, staying warm." He grimaced. "She apparently doesn't care for ice skating. I guess I'm not a very good boyfriend. I probably should have done something she wanted to do. But Wesley asked and I couldn't bring myself to say no."

"Oh, boyfriend." She frowned. "Then it's probably not the best idea to buy another girl hot cocoa, wouldn't you think?"

"I guess not. I'm sorry. My brain doesn't seem to be working too well today. At least, not around pretty girls." He winked.

"Now you're flirting." Holly looked as though she were fighting a smile.

Randy shook his head. "A terrible habit." He reached out his hand again. "I'm Randy, by the way." He chuckled.

"I know. I think we *may* have met before." She shot a teasing wink.

"Oh, we have? I must be a lucky guy then." He lifted his eye brows twice. "It's not every day a beautiful woman remembers my name."

"I'm sure your *girlfriend* does."

Ouch. Yeah, he deserved that. Why was he standing here on the ice flirting with Holly anyway? It wasn't like he was on the market or anything. But he couldn't seem to stop himself. Holly had him captivated. He didn't want to part ways with her. "Do you enjoy ice skating?"

"This is actually my first time. Which is why I haven't ventured very far from the wall."

"Oh, your *first* time? Really?"

"Yeah."

"Are you having fun?"

"I am, actually." Her smile widened.

"I can help you learn, give you lessons…if you'd like?" *Please say yes.*

"I…" She swallowed and glanced toward the small room where he'd said Lisa awaited. "I don't think your date would appreciate that."

"She's so buried in social media right now, I don't think she'd even notice, honestly. Besides, we're friends, right?" He held out a hand.

She stared at it and shook her head.

"I promise I won't try to kiss you or anything." Not that he wouldn't be *thinking* about it. What had come over him? His thoughts were completely inappropriate for someone already in a relationship. But perhaps that relationship needed to end. Sooner rather than later.

Her eyebrows shot up. "You won't unless you want an elbow in your gut."

"Ouch, you're vicious. But something tells me it might be worth it?" Yeah, flirting again. "But, thanks for the warning though."

She turned and began to slowly skate in the other direction.

He quickly caught up to her, his hand proffered. "Come on. Just try it," he urged. "Unless…do *you* have a boyfriend?"

But she had said she was here with the singles group, so…

"No, I don't have a boyfriend. But that shouldn't matter to you since *you're* not available. Unless you're the type of guy who dates two girls at once. Which, in that case, I definitely wouldn't be interested. I'm not into that type of thing."

"No, I wouldn't do that. But, I mean, *if* I weren't seeing someone else, would you…do you think *you'd* go out with me?"

She giggled. Or perhaps it was more of a chuckle. "Maybe."

"Maybe." He nodded. "Okay, maybe's good. It's not 'no,' right?"

Besides, if Holly lived around here, and he took a job in the area, his parents would be thrilled. Lisa had talked about them moving up north, closer to her parents, if they ever married. It wasn't that Lisa wasn't a nice girl—she was—but he didn't think "nice" had the makings of happily ever after like what his brother and sister-in-law seemed to be sharing. Not that he was all that sure about Holly, but he would like a chance to get to know her better. They'd seemed to have a few things in common so far.

However, prior to pursuing a relationship with Holly, he'd need to have a chat with Wesley. If the two of them used to date, that could pose a problem. How would Shannon feel about her brother-in-law bringing her husband's ex-girlfriend into the family?

Randy suddenly noticed a hand waving directly in

front of his face, and he blinked. "Sorry…Did you…were you saying something to me?"

"You really are out there, little brother." Wesley bumped his shoulder.

"Wesley. I thought…" He glanced around but the vision of loveliness had disappeared. "Where did she go?"

His brother frowned. "She's in the room over there, remember? You know the one where people rent the ice skates?"

"No, no. Not her."

"Who? Are you sure you're okay, little brother?"

"Yes, I'm fine. Where is Holly?"

Wesley frowned. "Holly?"

"The girl you used to date. Holly Remington. She was here. We were talking. I sort of crashed into her." Or maybe *crushed* into her would be more accurate. Because he definitely had a crush on her.

"Oh, she was? I hadn't noticed." His brother hadn't seemed to notice much of anything since meeting Shannon. He'd been on a cloud most days, especially since their baby arrived last year. Randy enjoyed being an uncle, but it likely didn't compare to having your own kid, he supposed.

Randy spun around slowly, surveying the rink for Holly.

"I think I saw a group of people head out to the parking lot."

"You did? Ah, man, I missed her."

"What…why? I think I'm missing something here."

"I asked her out."

"You—*what*?

"I mean sort of. Not really." He shook his head.

Wesley held a hand up to Randy's forehead. "Are you sure you're feeling okay, brother?"

Randy shoved his hand away. "I'm fine. I just…I like her. Like *a lot*. I mean…she's hot. And adorable. And—"

"Randy, you have a girlfriend!" Wesley frowned.

"I know."

"That you brought *home* with you from college."

"I know." Guilt ate at him.

"That you brought with you *tonight*—on a *date*."

"I know," he moaned.

"I thought…" Wesley shrugged. "I guess I don't know what I thought. But I would think that bringing a girl home for Christmas would, you know, kind of mean something special."

"I know. I just…I guess I'm changing my mind about Lisa."

"Why? She seems nice. You can't just do that to a girl, little brother."

"Okay, please stop with the *little brother*. You make me feel like I'm two years old."

"My point's the same."

"She's not my soul mate."

Did Wesley just snort? "Your soul mate."

"I don't know how to describe it. I just feel like I had this instant connection with Holly. I've never felt that way about a girl before."

Wesley nodded. "I get it. I understand completely."

"You do?"

"Yes, little brother. That's exactly how I felt when I met Shannon."

Excitement ricocheted through his chest like fireworks exploding. "Are you serious?"

Wesley laughed.

"She's *the one* then, right?"

His brother shrugged. "Maybe."

"But you said…never mind. Okay, I need her phone number. Like *right now*."

"Whoa. Slow down there, little brother. I think you have something to take care of before you go diving head first into another relationship." He motioned toward the waiting room.

"I know. I will. I'm taking her back home tomorrow."

"You're cold, man. You don't want to like wait till after Christmas and slowly break the bad news to her?"

"Why would I do that when I *know* Holly is the right one?"

"It's just…Lisa could already have dreams of marrying you. Something like this can be devastating for a girl."

"Oh." He paused and frowned. "It can?"

"Yep."

"Then what should I do? I mean, it's not my *intention* to hurt her."

"Pray about it."

"Pray. You're serious?"

Wesley rolled his eyes. "Yes, I'm serious."

"Okay, I can do that."

Wesley shook his head. "How many girls have you dated, Randy?"

"How many?" He frowned, then shrugged. "I don't know. At least a dozen or so."

"I wasn't referring to just the girls in high school."

He shoved his brother. "Okay, maybe a few more. I haven't been dating all that much in college. Too much bookwork to do."

"You do realize that Holly hasn't really had that many boyfriends. At least, not since I've known her."

"I can't see how. She's a knockout."

"She's choosy." His brother eyed him carefully. "And pretty serious about her faith." Had there been a slight accusatory tone behind Wesley's statement, or was that just Randy's conscience bothering him?

He crossed his arms. "I'm serious about my faith." Why did he feel like he had to defend himself?

"Mm…hm."

"What's *that* supposed to mean?"

"How many times did you attend church over the last few years since you've been away at college?"

"Quit with the 'holier than thou' attitude already, Wesley."

"I didn't say a thing about myself. We're talking about you. Answer the question."

He shrugged. "Half a dozen, maybe. I didn't really feel comfortable going to places I didn't know."

"I see. And how often did you read your Bible?"

"Seriously, Wesley?" He hadn't been prepared for an interrogation.

"So, I'm guessing the answer would be…?"

"Rarely, okay? It was rarely." Randy gritted his teeth. "But that doesn't mean I'm not serious about my faith."

"I think Holly may see it differently, little brother. Faith without works is dead. There has to be fruit."

"Is she really *that*…Christian?"

"I have no idea how to even quantify that statement." Wesley frowned his disapproval. "Can someone be *too* Christian?"

"Well, yeah, I think so."

"How?" His brother challenged.

He shrugged. "By going to church a gazillion times a week. By not having a life."

His brother adamantly shook his head. "I don't think Holly's the right one for you then. Nope."

"What? Why not?"

"Like I said, *she's serious* about her faith."

"What's it to you, anyway? It's not like you didn't dump her and marry Shannon."

"We weren't even dating anymore when I met Shannon. But I do care about her. She's a friend and a sister in Christ. I don't want to see her get hurt."

"That's the pot calling the kettle black if I ever heard it."

"I had no intentions of hurting Holly. We just weren't right together. That's why I didn't court her very long."

"Court? Did you just say *court*? What is that, some Amish thing you picked up from Grandma and Grandpa Stoltz?"

"No. Her family believes in courting."

"What does that even mean?"

"No kissing. Or touching. Chaperoned dates, etcetera, etcetera, etcetera."

A slow smile spread across Randy's face. Surely his

brother was pulling his leg. "You're kidding, right?"

Wesley shook his head. "Totally serious."

His smile turned the opposite direction. "So, if we date…or *court,* then I wouldn't even be allowed to kiss her?"

"Nope."

"So, you guys *never* kissed?"

"Nope."

"Oh. Wow. You're not even joking, are you?" He had to admit that he took pleasure in the thought that Wesley hadn't kissed Holly. But…

"Nope." Wesley placed a hand on Randy's shoulder and seemed to be studying him carefully. "If you're *serious* about this, little brother, then pray."

THREE

olly sipped her tea as she and Mom sat in the living room enjoying the roaring fire. It was something they often did on winter nights. It usually included a book, but Holly's mind was too preoccupied to read right now.

"What are you smiling about?" Mom asked.

Holly turned abruptly at her mother's voice. "I had fun tonight."

"That's good. I'm glad you didn't sprain your ankle or anything."

"Yeah, me too. I did get knocked over though." She chuckled at the thought.

"Oh, no."

"It wasn't a big deal." At least, the getting knocked over part wasn't a big deal. But meeting Randy? Yeah, her poor heart was *still* pounding. Hopefully, Mom couldn't perceive it.

"What is that wistful look for?"

Holly shrugged nonchalantly. "I don't know. I just…I met someone." She couldn't hide her smile.

Mom quickly sat at attention. "Someone?"

"Well, technically we kind of already know him."

"*Him*?" Now Mom's curiosity was definitely piqued. "Who?"

"Do you remember Wesley's younger brother? Randy?"

Mom nodded slowly, hesitantly. "Those Stoltz boys are handsome young men."

"Yeah, they are." She couldn't hide her smile if she wanted to. She'd been over the moon when Wesley had approached her father to ask to court her a few years ago. But that hadn't worked out. Maybe Randy, though…

"But hasn't Randy been off at college?"

"I guess so."

"I don't think he's been attending a Christian college," Mom said. Holly heard the disapproval in her mother's voice.

Holly shrugged. "Maybe they don't teach his major at a Christian college."

Mom's head tilted. "What's his major?"

"Oh, I wouldn't know."

"I don't think that young man had a very good reputation in high school."

"What do you mean?"

"Do you remember your brother Jason's old girlfriend? Ansley?"

"Yeah. What about her?" She'd never say so, but she never cared too much for Ansley. She seemed too into herself.

"I'm pretty sure your brother mentioned that Randy Stoltz was the one who turned her head, causing their breakup." Mom's lips flattened. "He played the field."

Holly frowned, not sure what Mom meant by that. "Meaning…?"

"Let's just say he's dated a lot of girls. Not just Ansley."

That didn't surprise her in the least. Of course a handsome young man like Randy would have garnered lots of attention of the female kind. Especially if he attended public school.

"Maybe he's changed." Holly didn't know why she'd said that. Just the fact that he'd brought a girl home from college *and* he was flirting with *her* when his girlfriend wasn't around, was enough to know that he *hadn't* changed.

"I suppose he *could* have. It's not likely though." Mom was right, of course.

But everything about him appealed to her. He was kind, handsome, funny. Handsome.

"Did he ask you out?" Mom's voice shook her out of her daydreaming.

"Um, he kind of had a date with him."

"I think I'm missing part of this story."

And, of course, she wasn't about to share everything with Mom. She just wouldn't understand. "She wasn't on the ice. She was on her phone in the skate rental room. He sort of crashed into me and we started talking. I enjoyed his company."

"He's not the right boy for you, Holly, if that's what you're thinking."

Her lips turned down. "How do you know?"

"Do you want a husband who's dated, kissed, and possibly been with a bunch of different girls? A man who, by the sound of it, might not be faithful?"

"We were just talking, Mom." Well, technically, they were flirting with each other most of the time. But Mom didn't need to know that. *Had he been with a bunch of different girls?* The thought unsettled her.

"Uh-huh."

Holly sighed. She'd never been so attracted to someone in her life, not even to Wesley. But Mom was right. Randy was clearly off-limits. Likely someone who would use her and break her heart. And after her brief courtship with Wesley, she wasn't sure she could endure another Stoltz brother heartache again.

Oh, but she was sure she'd be dreaming about Randy tonight. She wondered if he'd be dreaming of her as well. She secretly hoped so.

Several hours later, Randy lay in the darkness, staring up at the ceiling of his bedroom. *Pray… Pray… Pray…*

He was a coward, plain and simple. Not only had he not even begun to pray about Holly, but he'd failed to break up with Lisa.

Maybe Wesley was right. Maybe he *should* wait until after the holiday. But if he did, he wouldn't be able to spend any time with Holly during his winter break. He'd go back to school for his final semester, then she'd likely forget he even existed. Maybe even find someone else.

He couldn't let that happen. If he broke up with Lisa, he could at least spend the rest of his winter break getting to know Holly better. Then if they hit it off, they could communicate by email or text or phone or old-fashioned letters, even. For some reason, he got the feeling she'd enjoy the letter thing.

Yeah, it was selfish of him, but he craved Holly's attention. He'd thought of little else since they'd met.

Holly Remington. Even her name was gorgeous.

That was it. He would break up with Lisa. Right now. It wasn't fair to string her along when his heart and mind were clearly fixed on Holly.

He hopped out of bed and shuffled down the hallway in his socks. Hopefully, Lisa hadn't fallen asleep yet. He quietly knocked on her door, not wanting to awaken his parents. Mom would think he was trying to get away with something, sneaking to Lisa's room after everyone else had retired for the evening.

But nothing could be further from the truth. In his mind, he'd already relegated Lisa to the friend zone.

"Lisa," he whispered into the door's crack. "Are you still up?"

He heard shuffling, then Lisa opened the door a smidgen. "Randy?" She yawned. Probably a light sleeper.

Great, he'd woken her up. "Can we talk?"

"Now?"

"Yeah, in the living room. I have something on my mind." He led the way. Hopefully the setting with the crackling fireplace wouldn't seem like a romantic gesture. Perhaps he should have suggested the kitchen table instead. Oh well.

On second thought. "Uh, how about if we sit at the table?"

She looked toward the cozy hearth. "The table? It's warmer here."

"Yeah, okay. Here's fine." He just wanted to get this over with. He waited until she sat down, then he settled on a chair a couple of feet away.

"You wanted to talk?"

"Uh, yeah. About us. I mean…" He blew out a breath and raked his fingers through his hair. This would be much easier if she wasn't smiling. As though she were expecting him to say something wonderful. Because he wasn't. At least, it wouldn't be from *her* perspective.

"Yes?"

"What I mean to say is I…I…I'm sorry."

She frowned now. "Sorry? For what?"

"I don't think we're going to work out, you and me."

"What do you mean? What…did I do something wrong?" She swallowed.

"No, no. Not at all. You're fine." He stood up and began to pace the floor. "It's me. I'm…I'm kind of interested in someone else."

"Someone else?" Tears sprung to her eyes. *Not* what he wanted to see happen. "Really? You brought me all the way over here just to break up with me?"

"No. I didn't have in mind to break up with you when we left college. I just…I met someone else. Well,

I didn't really meet her. She's actually an old acquaintance and a friend of the family."

"So, you've been sneaking out to meet other women while we've been here?" Her voice screeched.

"No. I just, I ran into her." Literally.

Her arms latched firmly over her chest, her gaze accusing him of lying through his teeth. "When?"

"Tonight. At the ice skating rink. It was all quite by accident."

"Well that makes me feel much better, Randy." She rolled her eyes. "I should have listened to Misty. She was *so* right about you."

He didn't even know who Misty was. But it didn't really matter. "Would you like me to take you back home tomorrow?"

"Yeah, fine, whatever." She brushed away her tears.

"For what it's worth, I *am* really sorry. I never intended for this to happen. Someday, when you meet the right person, you'll thank me for this." Yeah, he sounded like an insensitive jerk, even to his own ears. He blew out a breath. "We can still be friends, right?"

"Please, just stop talking now. I'll pack my bags tonight." She jumped from the couch and scurried down the hallway back to the guest room.

Okay, so "no" to the friend question.

Now, he'd just have to endure the three-hour drive

up north to drop her off at her parents' house. He wasn't looking forward to it in the least, especially since tomorrow was a Sunday. But honestly, he couldn't wait to get back home and attend church with his family. If he and Lisa left at the crack of dawn, maybe he could make it back in time for the evening service.

And he'd have plenty of time to pray on the three-hour trip back.

FOUR

olly stared down at the hymnal as the congregation sang the second song of the evening service. She'd been disappointed that Randy hadn't showed up for services today, but maybe it was better if she didn't see him.

Perhaps his girlfriend hadn't wanted to attend. Which meant they were likely at home. Alone. Doing who knew what. Her heart clenched at the thought.

But she shouldn't judge. Judging had gotten her into trouble in the past. For all she knew, they could be attending a different church. There was nothing wrong with that.

On the other hand, if he'd come with his girlfriend, it would at least be a good reminder for Holly that he was off limits. Because, after all the daydreaming she'd been doing lately, she *needed* a reminder. She had no business dreaming about somebody else's man.

Why was she even dreaming about him at all? He wasn't the type of man she wanted for a husband. Not if he had a reputation that even her mom knew about.

She bit her fingernail. She knew why he'd been on her mind, though. In spite of herself, she genuinely liked Randy Stoltz. He was, for lack of a better word, charming. And she'd never been flattered with so much attention from a handsome young man. He made her feel wanted. Desired.

She shook her head at her thoughts. She should *not* want to feel desired.

Just as the song leader began the final stanza, Holly's gaze swung to the church's entrance. Randy slipped in as quietly as possible and slid into the pew next to his brother and his family. She pried her eyes off of him and glanced back at the door. Had his girlfriend not come with him?

She noticed him lean toward Wesley and whisper something in his ear. Wesley whispered something back and they both smiled. It was at that moment that Randy glanced her way, lifted a hand in greeting and sent her a smile that made her knees weak.

She grinned, but quickly ducked her head. Out of all the people in attendance, he'd sought *her* out. How would she ever be able to pay attention to the sermon tonight?

A sudden nudge from Mom caused her to jump. Mom frowned and nodded toward the pastor. Holly reached for her Bible beside her and opened it to the reference he'd mentioned. She'd attempt to keep her gaze riveted on the pulpit, but that would prove difficult. Especially since Randy had just caught her eye again, shooting a bold wink in her direction, causing her heart to flutter.

The moment the service ended, Randy made a beeline toward Holly. She was just as pretty as he remembered. Not that it had been a long time since he'd met her. Had that only been yesterday? It seemed like an eternity ago, gauging by how much he'd missed her—fantasized about her—since then.

But he was free now. No strings. Nothing holding him back. There was no reason they couldn't go out. Tonight. Unless she had other plans. He prayed she didn't.

"Holly." He knew his grin was as wide as Purdue's football field, but he couldn't suppress his excitement.

She smiled shyly, then turned to the older couple beside her. "Mom, Dad, you remember Randy Stoltz, right?"

Her father didn't say anything, but scrutinized him

from head to toe. It caused Randy to mentally squirm. What was the man thinking?

"Yes, it's nice to see you in church again, Randy." Her mother reached her hand forward and he shook it. "I'm Sue. And this is Bruce."

"It's been...how long since you've darkened the doors of this church?" Holly's father offered a slight nod, but skepticism still radiated from his being.

"I...uh...I've been off at college the past few years. I start my final semester in January." Hopefully that was nothing too worthy of judgment.

He was wrong. "Which Bible college have you been attending?"

He swallowed and glanced at Holly. He couldn't tell if she was enjoying this whole interrogation or if she was worried for him. He was definitely worried for himself. "I...um...it's not a Bible college. Purdue."

"I see." Her father frowned.

"What is your major, Randy?" Holly's mother spoke now.

"Civil Engineering." Should he have added "ma'am" to his reply? Randy looked to see her father's reaction. He didn't seem impressed. Most people would be. He wiped his clammy hands down his jeans.

"Oh, doesn't that involve a lot of math? I hate math," Holly said.

"We all have our strengths, honey," her mother encouraged.

"What kind of a job will you pursue once you've completed your education?" At least her father seemed a little interested now.

He blew out a relieved breath. "I'm not quite sure just yet. There are a variety of jobs that I'll be qualified for. I guess it depends on what's available."

"What would you like to do, Randy?" Holly's mother interjected.

He smiled. "I've thought about possibly designing toys."

"Toys?" Holly's grin widened. Good. She liked the idea too.

"Yeah, you know, educational toys that help grow the mind and inspire children to explore."

"Interesting," Holly's father said.

This conversation was taking way too long for his liking. "I...uh, Holly? May I speak to you for a few minutes?" He hoped it would be much longer.

She eyed her parents. Her father gave a slight nod. Was that a look of warning in his eye? What did it mean?

They moved to a quiet place in the sanctuary and dropped into an empty pew.

"Your parents are a little intimidating." That had

been the understatement of the year.

"They're very overprotective."

"Ya think?"

She smiled. "You wanted to say something?"

"Uh, yeah. Are you free tonight? Can we go hang out at Dairy Queen and talk?" *And maybe snuggle in my car?* No, that would *not* have been the right thing to say.

"What about your girlfriend?"

He shrugged. "We broke up. I told her I was interested in someone else. She's back home with her parents now."

"Wow, that was fast."

"I'm a fast kind of guy." Not the right thing to say judging by her expression. He was botching this up. Badly. "I mean, that didn't come out right. Sorry." He grimaced. "So…Dairy Queen?"

"Isn't it a little cold for ice cream?"

"I was thinking coffee. Maybe a burger and fries."

She frowned. "I don't think my parents would approve."

"Of Dairy Queen?"

"Of me going out with you."

"Why not?"

"Our family…we're a little more traditional. We don't really date."

"That's okay. I don't want to date your family. Just you." He teased.

She shook her head, but smiled in spite of herself.

"Okay, so what do I need to do to gain their approval? Because I'm obviously into you."

She ducked her head, probably trying to hide the beautiful crimson stain on her cheeks. He ached to caress them, maybe even kiss them.

Instead, he reached for her hand. But she pulled it away the moment he touched her.

He frowned. "No holding hands?"

She shook her head.

Disappointment ate at him. This was going to be a lot more difficult than he'd anticipated.

"You'll need to talk to my dad."

He frowned. "I just did."

"No. He'll want to interview you."

"*Interview* me?" He hoped his voice didn't just screech. Wesley hadn't been kidding. He glanced over to where his brother stood with his family. Wesley gave him an "I told you so" smirk. *Thanks, Wes.*

"He interviews every boy who's interested in me." She shrugged.

Every boy? He briefly wondered how many had been turned down. Turned away into a depressing heap of boyfriend wannabes. Would he be the next casualty cast upon the pile? "But you're…what…twenty-something? Can't you make your own decisions?"

"I'm twenty-three. And I believe my parents have my best interests in mind. I trust their judgment."

Why did he get the feeling the verdict would be a hearty "No!"? Maybe even with a boot to his backside. "So you're on board with all this?"

"I value my parents' opinion. But I make the final decision, since it's my future."

"Well that's good to hear." He looked up to see her parents making their way toward them. "Oh, no. They're coming. How can I...where can I see you?" Did he sound as desperate as he felt?

"I'll be here on Wednesday night for church. Our singles group meets here on Saturday at six. We're going caroling this weekend." Joy lit her eyes, then spread to her entire countenance. She was so beautiful he could hardly take his eyes off her. But he needed to.

A quick glance upward told him her parents had been detained by other congregants, praise the Lord. "I have to wait until Wednesday to see you?"

She tugged her bottom lip between her teeth, then leaned closer. "I'll be shopping at Walmart in Madison tomorrow. Probably around ten," she whispered.

His smile widened. Tomorrow couldn't come soon enough.

"But you still need to talk to my dad," she reminded him.

"Your father. Right," he said, as the subject of their conversation strolled up to them.

"Ready to go, Holly?" Her father cleared his throat.

Randy stood up. "I'd like to have a word with you, sir."

Her father eyed him and Holly, then moved a few steps away from where Holly now stood with her mother. "Say on."

"Um, I'd like to do the interview. To date Holly."

"You mean you're interested in *courting* Holly."

"Uh, yeah. Although, I honestly don't know what all that entails."

"No, I guess you wouldn't." Her father expelled a not-too-encouraging sigh. "We can meet before church on Wednesday, if that suits you."

"Before church, okay. What time?"

"Five o'clock."

"Okay." Randy held out his hand to shake her father's. "I'll be here then."

Her father offered a curt nod, then promptly left the building with his family.

Alrighty then.

FIVE

s soon as the coast was clear, Randy practically ran toward his brother. He grabbed Wesley's biceps, slightly shook him, and pleaded with him. "Wesley. You *have* to help me!"

Wesley chuckled.

"I'm serious. I'm about to go into the lion's den."

"Whoa, calm down, little brother."

He closed his eyes, attempting to keep what smidgen of patience he still had left. "Help. Me." He grounded out the words.

Wesley seemed to be having a hard time holding in a grin. "Okay, what do you want to know?"

"Everything."

"You don't ask for much, do you?" Wesley chuckled.

How could he be so carefree at a time like this? He wanted to shake some sense into his brother. Didn't he realize his little brother's future posterity was on the line? That he might not get a second chance at this?

"It'll cost you." Wesley's grin widened.

"Cost me?" Randy shook his head. "You're cold, brother."

Wesley shrugged. "They say to strike while the iron is hot."

"Okay, okay. What do you want?"

Wesley stroked his chin as though he hadn't a care—and had all the time—in the world. "How about free babysitting?"

"Babysitting?"

"At the rate you're going, you'll be needing it. Sooner rather than later."

"You're right. Okay, babysitting. When?"

"Wow, you just agreed with me."

"I think she's the one. I'm almost positive." He felt like shouting. Or making angels in the snow. Or—

"Okay, Saturday night."

"Nope. Can't do Saturday." Randy shook his head.

"Why not?"

"Singles group."

Wesley coughed, and amusement danced in his eyes. "*You're* going to the singles group?"

"Yeah, sure." He shrugged.

"Here? At church?"

"Is that so hard to believe?"

"Wow, Holly's already got you wrapped around her little pinky finger. And tied with a nice pink bow, by the look of it. This is going to be fun to watch." Wesley laughed.

"Just quit already."

"Okay, Friday then."

"I can do Friday. How long?"

"Hmm…let's see. If we go watch a movie—if anything decent is playing, then we go out to eat, and then maybe go bowling, and of course the drive into the city and back—"

"The city? You're going all the way to Cincinnati?"

"Well, I might want to take Shannon ballroom dancing or something."

"You're kidding. Please tell me you're joking."

"No joke, little brother. It's something Shannon's wanted to do for a long time. You should be taking notes, by the way."

Randy shook his head. "Okay, you have me all night. Whatever. Can we get on with this conversation already?"

"Okay. The *first* thing you're going to need to learn is patience. Watching Jaycee should help with that." Wesley chuckled.

"Why do I believe you?"

Instead of answering, his brother laughed. Again.

What on earth was he getting himself into? "You've changed a diaper before, right?"

"A *diaper*? I have to change diapers?!" Randy covered his eyes. This was turning into a nightmare.

Wesley shrugged. "Don't worry, Shannon can show you before we leave."

"But…she's a girl!" Was he sweating? Because it was beginning to get really hot in there.

"Yeah, that's kind of why I married her."

"No, I mean the baby."

"She won't bite…actually, I can't really promise that."

"Wesley," he growled out the word.

"You know what? This conversation is going to take a while. Why don't you come over tonight? We'll make some coffee."

"I prefer cocoa."

"Hmm…we might be out."

"Okay, coffee then."

"Come over around nine. The kids should be in bed by then."

"Nine. I can do that."

"On second thought, it might be better if you come around eight thirty. That way you can get some diaper training in."

If Randy had been holding something in his hands,

he'd be hurling it at his brother right about now. "I'll come at nine," he said through gritted teeth.

Holly stared out at the passing Christmas light displays from the backseat window of her parents' vehicle. She smiled to herself. She'd get to see Randy tomorrow. That was, *if* he showed up. But something told her that he would get to Walmart at ten o'clock in the morning if he had to walk barefoot through the snow. Okay, so maybe that was a little extreme. But he *did* seem eager.

After all, he'd broken up with his girlfriend. And he'd taken her all the way back home. All within *twenty-four hours* of meeting Holly. She'd never had someone show so much interest in her. It felt really nice, flattering. Like she was something special.

"What are you smiling about?" Her father eyed her in the rearview mirror from the driver's seat. "Don't put too much stock in the Stoltz boy."

She wanted to protest, but she wouldn't. She'd let Dad do his dad thing.

"I'm meeting with him on Wednesday before church," her father added. "But I don't want you to get your hopes up."

She nodded. Of course, she'd already known about the meeting because she'd been eavesdropping on their conversation. A terrible habit she needed to break. It would be easier if her hearing wasn't so good. Not that she wished to be hard of hearing. But she'd always been the curious type, which was why she loved working with children. Children were like sponges when it came to information, soaking up every minute detail.

She wouldn't let her father dampen her mood, although their meeting didn't seem too promising.

She wondered how Dad would react if he knew she'd mentioned Walmart to Randy. He'd likely be upset. But she felt Walmart was a safe place to see him. It wouldn't constitute a date. It was public and there would be plenty of other people around, especially since Christmas was just on the horizon.

Which brought her thoughts to caroling this Saturday night with the singles group. Even if Dad denied Randy's request to court her, they'd have plenty of opportunities to see each other through church activities. At least, until he went off to college. That alone was enough to make Dad deny his request. Did long-distance relationships ever work out? She supposed a few did, but the majority ended in failure. She thought she'd read about that somewhere. In the newspaper advice column, maybe?

Nevertheless, Monday, Wednesday, and Saturday seemed promising. She needed to start praying about Randy's meeting with Dad. Because if Dad agreed, well… No, she wouldn't get her hopes up. Not yet.

But Randy would definitely be in her thoughts, no doubt about it.

SIX

Randy shivered slightly and knocked on Wesley's door. He wasn't sure, though, whether his tremors were from the biting cold or nervousness. In many ways, he admired his older brother. He had everything. A good job, a nice home, a great wife and family whom he adored, a houseful of love.

Randy had never realized it until this moment, but this was *exactly* what he wanted. Maybe he *should* be taking notes from his older brother. He seemed to have it all together. Everything that mattered, anyway.

The door swung open. "Little brother, come on in before you freeze to death."

"So you're still calling me little brother, huh?"

Wesley shrugged and stepped aside so Randy could enter. "Force of habit. Must be all those pictures Mom has of me holding you."

Randy rubbed his hands together as they walked

through the kitchen. Sweetness lingered in the air, like Shannon had recently baked something tantalizing. He wanted a wife to bake him tantalizing treats.

Whoa! Where did that *thought come from?* Randy shook himself. "Let's get down to business?"

Wesley thrust a mug of coffee into his hands and he took a sip.

"Any yummy treats?"

"We may have a few cookies left if the kids didn't devour them all. I'll check." He gestured toward the living room, where Randy took a seat. "You may as well get comfortable. We're going to be here for a while."

"Not too long, I hope. I need my beauty sleep."

Wesley chuckled. "Got a big date tomorrow?"

He couldn't hide his smile if his mouth was plastered with duct tape. "Something like that. Holly's going to be shopping at Walmart. Ten A.M." He winked, accepting a paper towel containing two freshly-baked chocolate chip cookies.

"Did she tell you that?" Wesley's surprised expression elicited a chuckle.

"She *may* have mentioned something." He sat up prim and proper and feigned innocence.

"You have her breaking the rules already, little brother?" Wesley shook his head. "Not good. Not good at all. You're already a bad influence."

"She likes me. What can I say?" He scratched his chin, then his lips twisted. "Do you think I can get her to break other rules too?"

"You *are* a bad influence. I don't think you're going to survive the interview."

Randy moaned around a bite of cookie. "Why'd you have to remind me about the interview?"

"That *is* why you're here, right?"

Randy blew out a long breath. "Yeah, I guess so. Since I have no choice."

"Did you bring a notebook and pen?"

"What for?"

"You'll want to take notes."

Randy snorted.

"Okay, have it your way. Don't say I didn't warn you, though."

Randy cracked his knuckles, then leaned back against the couch. "Is it really that bad?"

"Okay, first of all, he's probably going to ask you what the purpose of the relationship is. What your intentions are."

"The purpose. Okay, I can handle that." He thought about it for a moment, then frowned. "What am I supposed to say?"

"The truth."

"Which is?"

"Think about it for a minute. That way you can come up with a coherent answer."

"Okay. The purpose of the relationship. Um, to take her out. Get to know her better."

"Ah…I guess that's a *start*."

"A start? What, am I supposed to have a speech written out by hand?"

"No. Typed, double-spaced on plain white paper. No mistakes." He chuckled.

"That's not *even* funny. I half believed you."

"Just consider the situation for a moment. He's looking for a worthy life mate for his daughter. Think of this from his perspective."

"Okay, I'll come up with *something*. Next?"

"He'll likely ask you about past relationships. And… how far you've gone." His brother eyed him warily.

"Oh, no. Past relationships? Oh, boy." His hands began feeling clammy and he wiped them on his jeans. And this was just his brother. "Can I lie?"

"Under *no* circumstances." Wesley nudged his shoulder. "And you should be ashamed for considering it."

This was discouraging. "Should I just forfeit, then? Because, by the sound of it, I'll be out of the running in the first round anyway."

"Just answer honestly. He might respect you because you tell the truth, even when you know it might harm your chances with Holly. There's something to be said for honesty."

"I don't know, Wes. I feel like he *already* hates me."

"He doesn't hate you. They're good people. If you get to know her dad a little, you'll see he's actually a friendly guy."

Randy grunted.

"We've all messed up," Wesley said. "Who hasn't?"

"You."

Wesley laughed. "Trust me, I've messed up plenty."

"But not in *that* department."

"Look, Randy. The most important part to him is not going to be how you've messed up in the past. It will be where you are spiritually, right now. What your plans are for the future—if it's with his daughter. Will you be a good husband? Are you going to pull her away from God or bring her closer to Him? Will you raise your children to love Jesus?"

"To tell you the truth, I want *this* for my future." He waved his hand around. "What you have."

"What you see here, brother, is the direct blessing of God. I followed His leading."

"Do you think I can have it too?"

"Maybe. If you put God first in your life. Get serious

about your faith, about serving Him."

"I'm not sure I know how to do that."

"You *are* saved, right?"

"Don't you remember when we got baptized in that pond in someone's backyard?"

Wesley nodded. "I remember. But getting baptized doesn't mean you have a relationship with God."

"I asked Jesus to save me when I was ten, if that's what you're referring to."

"And that's it?"

"What do you mean? I thought that was all there was."

"Well, yeah, that is all that's required for salvation. But when you get saved, it's called being 'born again' for a reason. You're like a spiritual baby, born into God's family. Babies need to be fed so they can grow. The Bible is the food new Christians need so they can mature in their spiritual life. If new Christians don't get fed, they will be weak and won't grow properly."

Randy grimaced. "Oh. I think I must have missed that part somehow."

"Too busy chasing girls, I'd venture to say."

Randy chuckled. "Yeah. You're probably right."

"That's what I meant by getting serious about your faith. Since Holly's been raised going to the church's school—and I think she might have been homeschooled too—then she's probably pretty spiritually mature."

Randy blew out a breath. "So, what you're saying is I'm behind. And I should start going to church regularly." Going to church would be a pleasure if Holly was there every time he attended.

"That's a good first step. If I were you, I'd start studying my Bible. And pray. God will lead you if you ask Him to." Wesley set his coffee on the table and leaned forward. "But don't expect your life to become perfect. It never is."

"Your life is."

"Hardly."

"How so?"

Wesley shrugged. "We fight sometimes."

"You and Shannon?"

He nodded. "It's not easy to provide for a family of six on my wages. I work. A lot. And I think sometimes Shannon gets lonely and craves adult company after being around the children all day."

"That's it?"

"No, there's much more. My point is that no family is perfect. But the good part about fighting with your sweetheart is you get to kiss and make up." Wesley smiled and winked.

"I'm going to enjoy *that* part."

"Just remember that words spoken in anger can be

forgiven, but they can never be revoked." He grimaced.

"You sound like you speak from experience."

"I've been a jerk at times. But I have a really, really good, loving, caring, understanding, patient, and forgiving wife. I don't know how she puts up with me sometimes."

"She realizes you're human."

"I'm definitely no angel."

"Well, I'm sure she isn't always either."

"She's a saint compared to me."

"I think you're being too hard on yourself. Because that's definitely not how other people see you."

"Wow, that's a compliment coming from you, little brother. Thanks."

"I said *other* people." He teased.

Wesley fake punched his arm and chuckled.

Back to the issue at hand. "So, what else is Holly's father going to ask me?"

"Probably about school, work, church, what you do in your free time. He'll be trying to get a good picture in his mind of who you are, basically. He'll want to know what kind of character you have."

Randy covered his face with both hands. "I'm doomed."

"I think *you're* being too hard on *yourself* now."

"It just seems like he's looking for perfection and

I'm so far below that… I almost feel like this is a hopeless cause."

"Like I said before, pray. You're putting confidence in yourself. Put your confidence in God and His plan. He knows whether you and Holly are meant to be together. If it's His will, *He* will make it work out."

"Okay, yeah." He expelled a breath. "I think I'll pray."

SEVEN

olly pushed her cart down an aisle of the local Walmart, occasionally adding items from her list. Mom had relegated this weekly task to her a couple of years ago, but she didn't mind. It gave her an opportunity to peruse the book section each week to see if any new titles had been released by her favorite authors. If she didn't make her quest a weekly adventure, there was a good chance the popular books would be sold out. The shelves didn't always get restocked, so she'd miss out if she didn't grab her copy right away.

She'd arrived ten minutes early, but hadn't spotted Randy's vehicle in the parking lot. She'd already glanced toward the entrance more than once, but she didn't want to seem too eager. But, man, was he handsome. He was so different than the boys she was used to. He seemed adventurous and spontaneous and carefree. The opposite of herself. But didn't opposites attract?

"Guess who?"

She'd been so wrapped up in her thoughts, she hadn't even noticed when the strong masculine hands covered her eyes. She smiled at Randy's voice and spun around.

"Fancy meeting you here." She couldn't seem to *not* flirt whenever Randy was near. Why was that? She wasn't one of those girls who flirted with all the guys.

"Hmm…" He eyed the book in her hand. "*The Cowboy's Forgotten Daughter*. Sounds interesting."

"Somewhat predictable, but they're good, clean stories."

The side of his mouth quirked up. "You lookin' for a cowboy, little lady?" he said with a twang in his voice.

"Why, I just might be." She splayed a hand over her chest and replied with her best Texan drawl.

"You wanna ride off into the sunset with me, darlin'?" he responded in kind.

She giggled. "It's an awfully temptin' offer, cowboy."

He let out a long sigh. "I'm really going to miss you when I go back to college." He was back to his normal voice now. "I'm tempted not to go back."

She gasped. "You have to. Isn't it your last semester?"

"Yeah."

"I'm sure it will go by fast. You'll probably be too busy to think about home."

He shook his head. "*You* is what I'll be thinking about. I've thought of little else since we crashed on the ice rink."

Her heart fluttered. She could get used to this much attention.

"I'm worried about my meeting with your father on Wednesday night. Do you have any pointers for me?"

She shrugged. "Just be yourself."

"That's what I'm afraid of."

"Why?"

"Well, I haven't always been the saintly person you see now." He chuckled.

"Everybody has a past. You learn, grow, and move on."

"Well, I'm glad you're forgiving."

She frowned.

"What is it?"

"My dad. He doesn't think we'll be a good match." She hated to put a damper on their conversation, but it was only fair that Randy know what he was up against.

"I already figured that. I've been praying now more than ever. Wesley's given me some good advice."

"Like what?"

"Like putting God first in my life. Getting serious

about my relationship with Jesus."

"Those sound like wise words."

"Well, you know my brother…" He let his words trail off.

"Yeah. About that…I think now I'm seeing a little more clearly why he and I didn't work out."

"Why do you think…?"

"Shannon." She stared at him. "You."

"Me. I like the sound of that." He smiled.

"God's plan for us is always better than our own. We can trust Him to do what's best."

He moved closer and lightly bumped her side, feathering his fingers over hers but failing to hold her hand. It was a deliberate teasing gesture that let her know he longed to do more.

The simple touch sent her heart galloping into the sunset. With her cowboy.

His intense gaze and quirked half smile made her almost wish he'd pull her to secluded place and kiss her breathless. She shook her head. She'd *definitely* been reading too many romance novels or watching too many romantic Christmas movies. Likely both.

She cleared her throat to redirect her thoughts. "Shopping."

A low rumble escaped his lips. Was there a thing he did that didn't add to his charm? She didn't think so.

"Do you have a list?"

She handed the paper to him.

"Ooh…I love spaghetti." His smile widened.

"You do?"

"One of my favorite things to eat."

She smiled. "Mine too. With extra parmesan cheese and garlic bread and salad."

"You're making me hungry." He eyed her. "Can you do lunch?"

"Uh…" She shook her head. "I probably shouldn't. There's a good chance someone's already seen us together here."

"Then why not lunch too?" His eyes pled. "I only have until the first, then I have to go back."

"I just don't think it's a good idea." She turned away from his probing gaze.

"Holly?" She turned toward him and he swallowed. "Is it because *you* don't want to or because of your parents?"

How could she answer that? Yes, she *certainly* wanted to. But spending time with Randy was dangerous. The more time she spent with him, the more that realization sunk in. They weren't courting. He wasn't even the kind of man she'd had in mind to marry. She wanted someone spiritually mature, who would guide their household in the ways of the Lord.

But she felt herself falling hard for him, in spite of that fact.

"Both. I mean, I do *want* to. I just don't think…I mean, my parents already wouldn't be happy if they knew that we'd arranged to meet today. I probably shouldn't have mentioned that I'd be here." She'd deceived her parents. What kind of an example was she being? Guilt ate at her.

His brow lowered. "I feel like I'm getting mixed signals here."

"I know. I'm sorry."

"Tell me what I need to do to be acceptable to you. I want you in my life. I want us to happen. But I don't know how to do that. Please. Give me a clue." She hated the hurt intertwined with his words. He seemed to be trying so hard to please her.

"It's not you, not really. It's just, we do things differently than the world."

Furrows etched in his forehead. "You sound like my Amish family."

"You have Amish family?" Her eyes widened.

"Yeah, my grandparents are Amish. My dad used to be, but left when he was a young man. He wanted a different way of life."

"Do you ever see them?"

"My grandparents?" He shrugged. "Occasionally.

Wesley knows them better than I do."

"Oh. Why is that?"

"Too much drama for me. You know, the whole shunning bit. It's ridiculous. People should be able to do whatever they wish. It's a free country. Why would anyone allow themselves to be manipulated and controlled like that?"

She could see she'd struck a nerve. But she had no idea what he was talking about. Her knowledge on the Amish was virtually zero. Now didn't seem like the right time to discuss the issue. And this certainly wasn't the place. "Maybe we can talk about that. Sometime in the future? You can write me when you're in college. If you have time."

"I could do that."

"Good. Now back to the issue at hand." She smiled. "I care for you, Randy. I want this to work between us—"

"You do?" She caught the excitement in his voice.

"I do. But we need to go about it in a good and honorable way. Do you understand?"

"So, no secret meetings?"

"No secret meetings."

"Wes was right. I *am* a bad influence on you." He chuckled.

She smiled. "Oh, I wouldn't say that. You are who you

are. That's part of why I like you. You're different."

His eyes sparkled with something akin to mischief. He leaned close and whispered in her ear. "I'd take your hand right now and kiss it, if you'd let me. Then I'd take each of your fingers and kiss—"

She abruptly stepped away, her heart fluttering. *How did he do that?* Just the thought of his lips on her skin, even if it was just her hand, made her breathless. But she couldn't let him continue lest she transform into tomato pulp right there in the store.

"I love to see you blush."

"I-I better finish my shopping," she stuttered.

"As you wish, little lady." He was back to his southwestern drawl again.

No, it was *not* as she wished. As a matter of fact, she fought very hard against what she wished to do right now. She *wished* she could abandon her shopping trip altogether and leave with Randy. Enjoy lunch together. Maybe walk down by the river together, holding hands and talking. Retreat to his warm car. Laugh together. Allow him to pull her close and, for the first time in her life, experience what it felt like to let a handsome young man press his lips to hers. To indulge in moments she'd only ever read about, dreamed about.

But she wouldn't. She couldn't. Not when Mom and Dad were trusting her to keep her pledge—to stay pure until marriage. Because Randy was the kind of boy, no *man*, who could get her into all kinds of trouble. And trouble only led to heartbreak. She'd seen it over and over again with her friends who dated casually. She'd already decided she didn't want that. Especially not with Randy. She wanted something deep, genuine. Not just superficial infatuation. *Real* love.

She needed to do better at guarding her heart. Because, at this moment, Randy Stoltz held it in the palm of his hand. And she wasn't so sure that was the safest place for it to be. If Randy broke her heart, she might not ever be able to recover.

A voice drew Holly's attention.

"Attention, everyone!" Randy had climbed up onto one of the metal DVD bins.

Oh no. Her eyes bulged. "Randy! What are you doing?" she called in a distressed but firm whisper.

Randy ignored her protests and continued his monologue. "See this beautiful young woman here?" He gestured toward her with his outstretched arm. "I'm falling madly in love with her."

"Randy!" She called out again in a whispered voice. "Stop."

She noticed other shoppers halt in their tracks, their attention riveted on the crazy guy standing a good four feet above everyone else. She moved behind one the aisles to hide, but peeked around the corner.

"I'm going to marry her someday," he continued.

She would have laughed if she wasn't so bewildered. What on earth was he doing?

"Uh, sir, you're going to need to get down from there." Holly heard one of the workers say.

Randy made a show of jumping down, and she heard the employee issue a stern warning about being escorted out of the store.

"I couldn't help myself," Holly heard Randy say.

A moment later, he caught up to her, a grin reminiscent of a crescent moon plastered on his face.

She shook her head. "What did you—"

A male voice from behind them interrupted. "It looks like my *gross sohn* might need some lessons on love."

Holly spun around to see an older Amish couple walking up behind her. The man seemed to be chuckling.

Did Randy know these people? Because she had no idea who they were. Had never met *any* Amish actually.

Randy's previous mirth immediately evaporated. His eyes narrowed. "If I need to learn any lessons on love, it certainly won't be from *you*."

Holly tried to process the scene in front of her. What was going on?

"I don't think causing a young woman embarrassment

in public is the best way to do it," the Amish man said, stroking his hoary white beard. An older woman in Plain attire accompanied him. They seemed pleasant enough.

"Like I said, I don't need or *want* your advice." Randy turned away from the man and looked at her. "Let's go, Holly."

"Uh, okay." She glanced at the older man apologetically, then followed Randy to another area of the store.

"I'm sorry about that," he said, once they were out of earshot of the Amish couple.

"Who was that?"

"Remember I mentioned my Amish grandparents?" He frowned.

Her jaw went slack. "And you don't get along with them…at all? I didn't realize…"

He shook his head. "I have no respect for them whatsoever."

Holly's eyes widened.

Randy continued, "They have treated my father poorly for most of his adult life."

"Why?"

"He's shunned. Remember I said he'd left the Amish when he was a young man?"

"I'm not familiar with the Amish. What does that mean exactly?"

"Well, for starters, he wasn't even welcome on their

property. They wouldn't even talk to him. He wrote them letters but they were returned unopened. They treated him like he was dead. Probably wished he was." He spat the angry words out. "They hadn't met my mom until a couple of years ago."

"Oh." She frowned. "Really? That's sad. Why?"

"Stupid religion."

"Randy." She shook her head. "You shouldn't—"

"Can we just change the subject, please? I do *not* want to talk about this right now."

She shrugged. "Yeah, okay. If that's what you want."

"I'm sorry. I didn't mean to spoil our time together."

She suddenly recalled the stunt he'd pulled just minutes prior, and couldn't hold in a giggle.

"What?" Randy's smile finally returned.

"You, that's what!" She pushed him playfully. "I can't *believe* you did that."

He laughed now. "I couldn't help myself. You make me crazy."

"Oh, so you're blaming *me* now." She fisted a hand on her hip.

"Oh, yes. It's *definitely* your fault. I'm usually perfectly sane."

"I can't believe you almost got kicked out of the store."

"It would have been worth it just to see that pretty blush on your face."

She hung her head, fighting a smile. "Do you, like, do this with every girl?"

"Only one." He winked. "Told you I'm crazy about you."

She laughed. "You're crazy alright."

Holly couldn't seem to get the interchange between Randy and his Amish grandparents out of her head. It was all she could think of as she lay in bed waiting for sleep to come. What had happened that made Randy lose all respect for his grandparents? They'd seemed friendly enough. But even if they weren't, they still deserved respect. Honor. For their position, if nothing else.

Randy's reaction to them bothered her. Big time.

How could he make a good husband to someone if he harbored bitterness in his heart? Didn't the Bible call bitterness a root? If that was true, then she'd have to dig deep to help Randy yank those roots out. Otherwise, it would spread and spoil other relationships in his life as well.

Holly didn't know how, but she was determined to help him. Maybe she would talk to Shannon about it. Did Wesley hold the same disdain for his grandparents? If not, why?

Although Holly and Shannon hadn't gotten along initially, they'd become fast friends once they worked out their differences. Holly had practically turned green the day Wesley Stoltz walked into church with Shannon and her siblings nearly two years ago. And seeing him with an adorable baby in his arms hadn't helped matters. But once she'd seen the error of her ways, and how perfect they were for each other, she'd gotten over her jealousy.

EIGHT

Holly closed the door to her room, sunk into the pillows on her bed, and scrolled her cell phone for Shannon's number. Perhaps her friend would have some insight into Randy's relationship with his grandparents. Had Shannon ever met them? Did she and Wesley get along with his Amish grandparents?

She shook her head at the thought of not getting along with one's grandparents. Maybe she'd just been blessed with two sets of good ones. She loved her grandparents dearly, and they in turn, cherished each of their grandchildren. And they had *a lot* of grandchildren to cherish.

"Hello?" Shannon's voice answered on the other end.

"Hi, Shannon. It's Holly. I've been wanting to talk to you about something."

"Sure. Do you want to come over? Or, better yet, I could meet you at the coffee shop in Versailles later. Wesley said he'd be home early today and I'm sure he wouldn't mind watching the kids. And I'd love to get out of the house for a few minutes. I could use a break."

Holly smiled. She could imagine needing a break when tending to small children full time. Her former employment at the daycare center had taught her that. "Okay. What time?"

"Let me talk to Wesley and I'll text you back. Will that work?"

"Sure. Any time is good for me. Just let me know." Holly disconnected and pondered the situation at hand.

Randy would be meeting with Dad tomorrow before church and she felt a little sorry for him. She didn't guess that Dad would go easy on him, but she suspected nothing was going to scare Randy away. He seemed like the kind of guy that would not give up easily if he didn't get his way. Was that a good or a bad trait to have? She supposed it could be either, depending on how it was implemented.

All she knew was that she needed to pray. Because if Randy wasn't who God had planned for her, she didn't want to begin a relationship with him. But hadn't she already? She knew how she felt when Randy was around. Vibrant and full of life. And aside from the confrontation with his Amish grandparents, he seemed to always have a smile on his face. Granted, it was usually a mischievous smile, but a smile nonetheless. And she didn't doubt that she smiled quite a bit whenever she was in his presence as well.

Could her happily-ever-after be with Randy Stoltz? Or was this mirth just a temporary circumstance that would eventually lead to heartache?

Her phone vibrated and she glanced down at the message.

Can you meet me in thirty minutes?

She quickly texted Shannon back. *I'll be there.*

Twenty-five minutes later, she rolled to a stop in front of the small café. She didn't come here too often, but when she did, she loved it. It reminded her of some of the coffee shops she'd read about in books. Many times, it was where the main protagonists met for the first time or where they connected. She wondered if Randy ever stopped in here to indulge in something delicious.

And there she went, thinking of Randy again. She was hopeless.

Shannon pulled up beside her in an SUV and waved.

Holly stepped out of the car and they briefly embraced one another in greeting. "Whatever you want. My treat." She grinned.

Shannon smiled. "Must be my lucky day. Unfortunately, I can't indulge in coffee right now." She rubbed her flat abdomen.

Holly's eyes expanded. "Are you expecting again?"

Shannon nodded and put a finger to her lips. "You're only the second person I've told."

She guessed the first must have been Wesley. "Your secret's safe with me."

They walked toward the entrance and stepped into the cozy establishment.

"We want to tell Wesley's parents and the kids at Christmastime. It'll be a nice surprise for everyone."

"I'm sure they'll be thrilled." Holly inhaled deeply. "I just love the smell in here. It's inspiring, isn't it?"

Shannon laughed. "I guess I've never thought of a café as inspiring."

"I just think it would be the perfect setting for a book."

"You like to read a lot, don't you?"

Holly nodded and they placed their order with the barista.

"I enjoy it too, but I have so little time. And with a

husband and kids, I feel like I rarely have the energy to do anything else but keep the household going."

They found a seat on a small sofa. "Are you usually low on energy? Because my mom swears by blackstrap molasses."

Shannon's face wrinkled. "Blackstrap molasses?"

"Yeah. I guess it's really good for getting your iron up."

"I do usually get low on iron when I'm pregnant. At least, I did with Olivia."

"She's a little doll, isn't she?"

"She is, but she's into everything now that she's walking. And then her and Melanie together? It's impossible to keep the house from looking like a tornado blew through. Wesley's very understanding, though, and he's a big help."

"That's good. He always seemed like a good guy."

Shannon smiled knowingly. "So what's this I hear about you and Randy?"

Holly couldn't hide her smile. "What do you think of him?"

"Randy? He's a big kid. He's fun. The kids love their Uncle Randy."

Holly frowned. Not exactly what she wanted to hear. Fun was good, but did that mean he was irresponsible? She shook off the thought. "He does seem to have the ability to make people smile." Except her father.

Their order was up. Holly quickly retrieved their drinks from the counter and offered Shannon's tea to her with a couple packets of honey.

"Thanks." She smiled. "Was there something specific you wanted to talk about?"

"Yes, actually. Do you know Randy's Amish grandparents?"

Shannon's smile grew large and a look of fondness passed over her features. Nothing like Randy's reaction. "I love his grandparents, *Dawdi* Christopher and *Mammi* Judy."

"And Wesley does too?"

"Oh, yes. They actually had a hand in getting Wesley and me together, sort of."

"Really?"

"It's a long story, which I'm sure you'll hear one day. But Jaycee mistook *Dawdi* Christopher for Santa Claus." She shook her head. "Apparently, Jaycee had climbed up in his lap while he was waiting for *Mammi* Judy and told him what he wanted for Christmas."

Holly laughed. "Are you serious?"

"Dead serious." She took a sip of her tea. "And then a week or so later, they showed up on our doorstep bearing gifts."

"That sounds so sweet." She shook her head, imagining it all. "And Wesley came with them?"

"No. Wesley and I met at the restaurant I used to work at. It wasn't until later that I discovered they were related. It was certainly one of those 'it could have only been God' moments."

"Wow. So, Randy? He doesn't get along with them?" Shannon frowned. "Why do you ask?"

"Well, we ran into them in Walmart the other day. It wasn't a happy exchange."

"I think Randy must've been hurt at some point in time. At least, that's my guess. Because I think there's more to it than their father being shunned."

"Yeah, he'd mentioned the shunning."

"I think maybe Randy may have shut off a part of himself. He acts like it's no big deal, and brushes it away claiming he doesn't want to get caught up in all the, and I quote, 'Amish drama.' But I really think he's hurting."

"I thought it might be something like that." Holly frowned.

"We all deal with things our own way. I think his being angry with them is how he copes."

Holly nodded. "I was shocked at his reaction to them. He wasn't very respectful."

"Yeah. He pretty much avoids them during the holidays, which I think is sad. Wesley's just glad that they're coming around more now."

"And how do their parents feel?"

"They're grateful. *Dawdi* Christopher and *Mammi* Judy are really taking a risk when they visit. I think they do it in secret."

"Oh." Holly frowned, sipping her light decaf soy mocha. "Really? Why?"

"Well, it goes back to the whole shunning thing. It's supposed to make those who left want to return. But I think they finally see that that isn't going to happen with Wesley and Randy's father. And instead of losing out on that relationship for the rest of their lives, they stepped out in faith—and against their church's *Ordnung*—and offered the right hand of fellowship to them."

"*Ordnung*? What is that?"

"That's the ordinances, or rules, that the church members are required to follow."

"Oh."

"You know, that's why they dress conservatively and drive a horse and buggy. Those are all rules they have to abide by."

"Okay, I see. So they *have* to dress that way?"

"Yes. It isn't an option."

"I always wondered. I never met any Amish people until at Walmart yesterday. And, technically, I didn't even meet them. Randy and his grandfather exchanged a few words and then we moved to a different area of the store."

"I find it interesting that you and Randy were at the store together."

"Oh, we weren't together. We just sort of met there."

Shannon nodded slowly.

Holly leaned over. "My parents don't know that we saw each other."

"I was wondering about that. Isn't he supposed to talk to your father at church tomorrow?"

"He is. How did you know?"

"He came over to us as soon as you left the church. He begged Wesley to help him."

Holly laughed, as her cheeks heated. Was it the coffee or the realization that Randy had taken such an interest in her?

"He really likes you." Shannon smiled.

"I don't know why." She shrugged.

"Don't sell yourself short. You're really sweet and very pretty."

Holly hung her head at her friend's praise. "I don't know about that."

"I was a little jealous the first time I saw you." Shannon laughed.

Holly shook her head. "You had reason to be. I was still pining after Wesley back then. I can't believe the way I acted. I'm so embarrassed by it now."

"That's been long forgiven."

"I wish I could forget." She rolled her eyes.

"Well, you weren't the *only* one who acted silly."

"I know. But *I* knew better."

"What do you think your father will say?"

"About Randy?"

Shannon nodded.

"I don't know. He can be rough."

"He loves you." A slow smiled formed on her lips. "You are fortunate to still have your parents living."

She thought of Shannon and her siblings, who'd lost both of their parents just a couple years ago. She couldn't even fathom the responsibility laid upon her friend's shoulders at the tender age of eighteen. Wesley had truly been a Godsend for the Parker family. Holly hadn't seen it then, but it was crystal clear now. "I know. I'm sorry your parents are no longer here."

"I miss them so much sometimes." Shannon blinked back a stray tear, then straightened.

"I can imagine."

"But I might not have met Wesley or his grandparents, had my parents not died."

"Yeah, I guess God has a way of making everything work out."

"And He will with you and Randy."

"I don't know if there will be a 'me and Randy'. My father is wise and I trust his judgement. I'm not sure Randy will meet his approval."

"So if he doesn't think you and Randy courting is a good idea, then what?"

She really didn't want to think about that until it happened, which it probably would. "We'll have to settle on being friends, I guess."

"And you're fine with that?"

No, she wasn't. Not really. "I have to be."

"Well, would your father make any concessions?"

"What do you mean, specifically?"

Shannon shrugged. "Would he allow you to write letters to each other while Randy's in school?"

Holly grimaced. "Maybe. But I wouldn't hold my breath."

"But while he's here, you can see each other at church, right?"

"Yeah."

Shannon eyed her carefully. "Would you ever go against your father's recommendation?"

Holly took a deep breath. Hadn't she been asking herself the same thing? "I really like Randy."

"And…?"

She swallowed the remainder of her mocha. "If my father says no, I will try to forget about him."

"You have a lot of respect for your father. I admire that."

"It's not always easy. But I know he has my best interests in mind. He loves me and only wants good for me. I have to trust him."

"It's the same with God, isn't it? Our *Heavenly* Father. We trust Him because He loves us and only wants what's best for us."

"Yeah, you're right. That's exactly how it is. But God is all-knowing and He never makes mistakes or misjudgments."

"Are you worried that your father could misjudge Randy?"

"Not really. I just don't think Randy is at the place, spiritually speaking, that my father would approve for a life mate. You know what I mean?"

"Yes. And he's probably right. Randy is a nice guy, but I've never seen him show much of an interest in spiritual matters."

Holly frowned. "That's what I was afraid of."

"But on the bright side, he's eager to go to church since meeting you."

"Yeah, but it's the wrong reason."

"God can use wrong reasons." Shannon smiled. "Look at me. I went to church because of Wesley."

"You're right."

"Just pray that God will reach his heart. Wesley and I have already been praying for that. Randy meeting you might just be God's way of drawing him into the fold."

"Do you think he's saved?"

Shannon nodded. "Wesley says yes. He accepted Christ and was baptized as a boy."

"Well, at least the foundation is right."

"If he's going to church regularly, maybe he'll start growing up."

Thinking of Randy's behavior in Walmart, Holly eyed Shannon doubtfully. "I don't know. Maybe."

Shannon's cell phone vibrated and she stared down at it. "Oh no. Duty calls."

"Is everything okay?"

Shannon held out the phone toward her.

Holly gaped at a digital image of the two youngest children, Melanie and Olivia, covered in flour. Little Olivia wore the empty mixing bowl atop her head, but she was all smiles. The text from Wesley's number read *Miss you, Mommy!*

Shannon laughed. "I don't know who's missing me more—the children or Wesley. I'm afraid of what disaster may be awaiting me."

"Maybe you should send him a text letting know you're on your way. Then maybe they'll have most of it cleaned up."

"I'll be lucky if it's half cleaned up. I think I should stop in at IGA and pick up some extra paper towels. By the look of it, we're going to need them." Shannon looked at her phone, shaking her head. "What did he let them do?" She lamented.

"You should probably pick up more flour too, by the look of it."

"Probably." She stood from her seat. "By the way. Would you be willing to babysit for me Friday evening?"

"Friday?" She slung her purse over her shoulder. "Sure. What time?"

"Six thirty. We might be out late."

"That's fine."

"Thank you. I'll be sure to leave you a list of instructions. And the kids go to bed at nine, so most of the evening should be quiet."

"No problem. I love children." Holly smiled. She'd be sure to bring a book along for after the children retired for the evening. "It sounds like fun."

"Good." Shannon sighed. "Well, I'll see you at church tomorrow."

Holly waved as her friend slid into her vehicle then drove off.

NINE

Randy drove up to the church ten minutes prior to his meeting with Holly's father. He guessed her father was likely a stickler for punctuality, so he didn't want to start off on the wrong foot. Being on time was something Randy was actually good at. He was rarely late, and when he was, it couldn't be helped. Like showing up late to church last Sunday evening because he'd dropped Lisa off.

He parked the car and wiped his sweaty palms on his jeans. *Oh no.* Should he have worn slacks instead? Would Holly's father approve? He should have asked her. Or Wesley.

Had he ever been this nervous? He didn't think so. This was way worse than a job interview. Or his first day of college. This was his chance to be able to spend time with the girl of his dreams. He couldn't botch this up.

Please help me, God. He shot up the desperate plea.

It was the strangest thing, really. He'd never been this head-over-heals for a girl. Never. It had all been just fun and games up until now. But now? It was like he'd become a different person overnight. The moment he bumped into Holly at the ice skating rink was like he'd been struck by lightning. His world shifted. Or perhaps the stars had been perfectly aligned that night—whatever that meant. Either way, it was as though his feet started down a different path.

All of a sudden, he wanted to be a different person— a better person. He wanted to be who Holly needed. Who her father approved of. Someone worthy of her affections, of her love.

He tapped on the steering wheel, then glanced down at his watch. Her father was late. So maybe he wasn't a stickler for punctuality.

He sucked in a deep breath as a vehicle *finally* entered the parking lot. At five twenty. He could have sworn Holly's father had told him five o'clock. Maybe he'd been mistaken. Had he said five thirty?

Randy exited his vehicle, contemplating if it would be better to meet Holly's father at his vehicle or at the door of the church. He opted for the latter.

His heart rate sped up as Mr. Remington approached. *What was his name?* Randy squeezed his eyes shut, attempting to recall it. He could kick himself right now.

He held out his hand. "Mr. Remington."

Holly's father shook his hand and nodded. "I see you're here on time."

"I was actually early. I was here at ten till."

Mr. Remington didn't reply, but instead unlocked the door to the church.

Randy frowned. *No apology for being late?*

Holly's father led the way into the church's fellowship hall, and Randy took a seat across from him at the table.

Randy rubbed his palms on his jeans. He couldn't wait for this to be over.

"How old are you, Randy?"

Yes, an easy question. "Twenty-one."

"And you consider yourself a Christian?"

"I do." Although he would admit he hadn't been living like it, if her father asked.

Mr. Remington studied him. "Do you drink alcohol?"

His mind went back to a frat party he'd been invited to a couple of years ago. He'd drunk so much, he had passed out. When he woke up, he'd been so sick he thought he was going to die. He'd missed all his classes that day. Since then, he'd indulged in a drink here and there with friends, but he'd never been wasted like at the party. And he never wanted to be again.

"I have. I do, on occasion," he admitted. "My parents don't approve."

"Are you willing to give it up or do you plan to bring it into your marriage?"

"I guess I've never contemplated that." He shrugged.

"Are you aware of what the Bible says about alcohol?"

His brow lowered. "Uh…it's okay to use it for sickness?"

"Surely you've read the story of Lot."

"Sodom and Gomorrah, right?"

"I'm thinking of what happened after that."

Randy was drawing a blank. "I'm not sure what you mean."

"You can read about it in Genesis nineteen. Basically, he got so drunk that he didn't even realize he'd gotten both of his daughters pregnant."

Eww. He grimaced.

"Do you remember the story of Noah?"

"He got drunk too, didn't he?"

"Yes. And his sons found him in his tent. He ended up cursing one of his sons. I think it's interesting that the Bible doesn't record anything positive about his life after that incident."

"Hmm…I guess I've never thought of that."

"The book of Proverbs says that *wine is a mocker and strong drink is raging, and whosoever is deceived thereby is not wise.*" He frowned. "I realize that drinking alcohol has become an acceptable part of our society, even in many of our Christian circles. I do not hold to or agree with that view. Alcohol has caused much harm and heartache. It is not a burden I wish for my daughter and her future family."

Randy thought about Sean Perry, a high school acquaintance he'd had in one of his classes. Sean and his sister were both killed when a drunk driver swerved into their lane and hit their vehicle head-on. Their younger sister survived, but she'd gone through many months of surgeries and still dealt with the consequences of the drunk driver's fatal decision to get behind the wheel that day.

"I'm willing to give up alcohol, if you think I should. I enjoy it, but it's not that important to me."

"No, Randy. It must be a decision *you* make. *My* decision is based on my convictions and my desire to lead my family in righteousness. My decision is based on setting a good example, not only for my children, but for my future grandchildren as well. Everything we do will affect other people's lives whether we realize it or not. God forbid I should become a stumbling block to those I love and cherish most."

Randy considered his words and nodded.

"Do you have any addictions?"

He scratched his head. "No. Not that I know of."

"I don't expect perfection, Randy, and neither does my daughter."

"That's good to know."

"But what I *do* expect is a desire to live righteously before God."

"I haven't always wanted to, but I've been seeing things through new eyes lately. An actual relationship with God is still a pretty new concept to me. I don't know all the ins and outs, but I'm willing to learn."

"I see." Mr. Remington nodded. "And your relationship with my daughter…"

Randy swallowed. Now he was getting down to business.

"If you court my daughter, where do you see your relationship a year from now?"

"A year? I would hope Holly and I would be pretty serious a year from now."

"What does *pretty serious* look like to you?"

"Thinking and talking about marriage."

"And how about physical contact?"

"Well, that would depend. Whatever Holly's comfortable with…" He shrugged, then lifted his eyes to Mr. Remington's frown. "I mean, not like whatever, but…" Now he'd gotten himself in a mess. *Whatever, Randy? Really?*

"And your past relationships? Did they include *whatever*?"

Was it getting hot in there? "That didn't come out right."

"Are you avoiding the question?"

Yes. "No. And yes, my past relationships have included physical contact."

"Beyond kissing and holding hands?"

"Yes."

A deep frown etched in his face. "I see." Holly's father blew out a long breath. "And you think you're worthy of my daughter?"

"Oh no. I'm not even close to being worthy of her. She's…amazing…and so far out of my league. If I'd known, if I'd been able to see the future, I totally would have waited for her." He squeezed his eyes shut and offered a silent plea. He was botching this up so badly. "I've done a lot of wrong things—stupid things—in my life. If I could go back and redo some parts, I would. But I can't. And this is where I'm at right now. I know I don't have much to offer, but if you'll just give me a chance, I'll try my best not to mess it up."

"Are you willing to meet with me for discipleship once a week?"

"Discipleship?"

"To help you grow in your walk with the Lord and

develop an understanding for the Word of God."

"That would be great. But I go back to college in early January."

"Are you able to take satellite classes for that?"

Randy frowned. Satellite classes? What a brilliant idea! But first, he'd have to see if there were any close by. "I think that's a wonderful idea." Plus, he'd get to see Holly more.

Her father nodded. "Why don't you take Sunday dinner with us?"

"Dinner? Like at your house?" His mind reeled with excitement, flip-flopping all over the place. Was he serious?

Mr. Remington smiled.

"I'd like that. Does this mean…?"

"Yes. But I have a list of things here that Holly has agreed to, that I'd like you to consent to as well. A code of conduct, if you will."

"A code of conduct?"

"I'll go over a couple with you. First of all, in order to protect your relationship and my daughter's reputation, you two are not to be alone in a room together." Her father eyed him.

Randy nodded, but his mind balked at the idea.

"Now, that doesn't mean there will be people around at all times listening in on your conversations. We just don't want to give place to the devil and open the door to temptation, which, if you're like most young men, is probably pretty strong." His brow rose in question.

"Yes, I will admit that."

"And with your background, it's likely stronger than it should be."

He considered the warning and nodded.

"And the second thing is no touching."

"Like…at all?"

"At all."

"No holding hands or—"

"At all."

There went his grand plan for Holly's ice skating lessons. He blew out a breath and acquiesced. "At all."

"It will be challenging."

"For sure." Randy glanced up at the clock. "May we sit together during church?"

"I think that would be okay. Just keep in mind the no-touching rule and you'll be fine. You'll be watched."

"I figured." He chuckled. "So, then I'm allowed to take Holly out as long as someone is with us? Like a double date?"

Her father nodded.

He said yes? He said yes! *I was approved. By Holly's father.*

He. Said. Yes.

Oh my.

Randy was so excited, he felt like running up and down the aisles, hopping on the back of one of the pews, and sailing through the air to swing from one of the hanging light fixtures. But the pastor and congregation probably wouldn't approve of that. And it could be costly if the light fixture were to come crashing down. It would be so worth it, though.

He said yes!

If only church weren't still twenty-five minutes away. If only Holly would show up early. He couldn't wait to share the news with her. And with Wesley. And with every other person who would lend him an ear and celebrate his good fortune with him.

He said yes.

TEN

*H*olly's heartbeat quickened with every mile closer to church. If only Mom would drive faster. Or perhaps she should have driven her own car. She surmised that either way, the drive would have taken forever.

She couldn't wait to see Randy. Ever since her father left home to go to his meeting with Randy, Holly had been on pins and needles. She wasn't all that optimistic at the outcome because she was quite certain Dad's response to Randy would be a big fat, "No!" Nevertheless, she'd been praying for God's will in the matter.

Whatever the outcome, though, she was still excited to see Randy at church tonight. She'd miss him miserably when he returned to college after the new year. Hopefully, they could write letters back and forth to continue their friendship.

The moment Mom's car rolled to a stop, Holly practically jumped out. Well, she tried to. She *would* have if she hadn't forgotten that her seatbelt was securely fastened. Stupid thing.

She attempted nonchalance as she drew the door to the church open. Her eyes immediately searched out Randy, who was chatting with her father in the second pew. As if he could sense her presence, his head turned toward the foyer. A handsome smile danced across his features and he rose from the pew and headed in her direction.

"Will you walk outside with me?" His smile belied his serious tone.

"Of course." She glanced back at her father, who was in the process of greeting Mom.

Randy held the door open for her and the two of them stepped outside into the brisk air. "Are you too cold? If so, we can go back inside."

"No, I'm fine."

"Let's sit?" He gestured to the bench in front of the church.

She sat down next to him, anxiously waiting to hear how his meeting with her dad went. It took everything within her not to shake him into spilling every minute detail.

A huge smile spread across his face.

That could only be good, right?

"If I were allowed to touch you, I'd take you into my arms and spin you around in circles. And maybe even kiss you." A lopsided grin formed.

She gasped. "He said yes?"

Randy nodded, his eyes sparkling. "He said yes."

"Really? I can't believe it."

"Neither could I. But he's giving me a chance, so I'm going to do my best not to blow it."

"Wow." She couldn't keep herself from smiling.

"I don't know how I'm going to do with this no-touching thing. I'm dying to lift my fingers to your face and caress your cheek."

Her cheeks heated at his blatant forwardness.

"Is there such a thing as speed courting?"

A giggle tripped from her lips.

He squeezed his eyes closed. "You know, this has to be a form of cruel torture. I want to kiss you so badly."

"You're so dramatic. And cute." What would it feel like to let him kiss her? She could only imagine.

"I am?"

She nodded.

"You're pretty darn cute yourself."

She needed to change the subject, focus their attention elsewhere. "I'm excited about caroling on Saturday. Are you?"

"I'm excited that I'll get to be with you."

"You don't like caroling?" She felt her lips turn down at the sides.

"Ah." He shrugged. "It's okay. I'm not the best singer in the world."

"That's fine. You can always lip sync if it's that bad."

He chuckled.

"I pretty much love everything that has to do with Christmas. It's definitely my favorite time of year."

He lifted his hand toward her face, then must've thought better of it, and dropped it to his side. "Guess what?"

"What?"

"I'm coming to your house for dinner on Sunday."

"You are? My dad invited you?" Excitement bubbled in her belly.

"Mm-hm."

Music wafted outside from the auditorium. "Oh, it sounds like we better go inside. Church is starting."

"I get to sit by you." He grinned.

They stood from the bench and he held the door open for her.

"I think I'll like that."

ELEVEN

A few moments later, Randy gestured toward the pew in front of Wesley and his family. He slid in beside Holly and she offered him a hymnal. Randy glanced back at his brother, his smile wide, and gave him a thumbs up. Wesley nodded in turn, seemingly impressed.

His brother leaned close and whispered. "You'll have to tell me all about it later."

"You know I will." Randy whispered back, then turned his attention to the song leader, who'd chosen a Christmas-themed song. He didn't miss Holly's smile or joyful exuberance as she sang with her heart and voice.

The service flew by way too quickly for his liking. It was a strange thing, really. As though just being next to Holly made him feel like a better person. Her enthusiasm for life and faith seemed to automatically rub off on him.

He had participated in the congregational singing more than he ever remembered doing. He listened intently to the pastor's sermon, occasionally glancing toward Holly, who'd been fervently jotting down notes and Scripture references. It was like a whole new experience. Nothing less than amazing.

Holly turned to him after the closing prayer. "I'm going to ask my parents if they mind staying for a while so we can talk."

"Okay." He nodded, then watched her walk in the direction of her parents.

He turned to Wesley. "Can you believe her dad agreed? I'm still trying to get over the shock."

"So, how are you going to manage with college and all that?"

Randy shrugged. "We'll figure it out." He thought on her father's suggestion of attending satellite courses. It was something he'd definitely need to look into. But even if that wasn't feasible, the thought of them corresponding by letter sounded exciting. He had a feeling that if he didn't attend a satellite campus, he'd be spending an awful lot of money on gas.

Holly returned. He'd almost grasped her hand, but caught himself. This whole no-touching thing was such a foreign concept to him. It would take some getting used to.

"Let's go sit in the back," he suggested.

"Sure." Her smile stretched across her face, telling him she might be as excited as he was about their courtship.

Wow, they were actually courting. Officially. Wouldn't his college buddies get a kick out of that?

She slid into one of the chairs at a table in the fellowship hall. He sat across from her, to avoid the temptation to touch her.

Randy's smile broadened and he caught Holly's eye. "Can you believe your father agreed? I'm still floored."

She loved his enthusiasm. It had certainly been an answer to prayer. But, what now? They seemed to have so little time together before he busied himself with his college courses again. Not a lot of time to build a relationship. She knew she'd miss him immensely while he was gone. And then there was added worry about all the college women he'd be around. The type of women Randy was used to. Women he could likely date and touch at will. Was she fooling herself, thinking the two of them could even make a relationship work? They seemed to be opposites in so many ways.

She snapped out of her melancholy thoughts.

Thankfully, Randy hadn't seemed to sense her volley of emotions. "You're still coming to caroling on Saturday, right? You're not going to back out or anything."

"And miss spending time with you? Do I look like a crazy guy?" He chuckled. "Wait. Don't answer that."

He never ceased to make her giggle. "What are you doing tomorrow?"

"I'm not sure. Your dad and I talked about the possibility of me attending college at a satellite campus. That way I'd be closer. I'll likely be researching for that."

Her smile widened. "Really? Is there one close by?"

"There might be one in Columbus."

Her heartbeat quickened. "That's only…what, like an hour away?"

"Or less. It would sure beat going all the way up to West Lafayette."

"When does it start up again?"

"The second Monday in January. Since it's my last semester, it's going to be pretty intense."

"But you'd be living at home, right?" She couldn't suppress her excitement at his announcement.

He nodded.

"I'll be praying for you."

His lips twitched.

"What?"

"You're cute, that's what." He winked.

"I've never considered offering to pray for someone to be 'cute.' I take my prayers seriously."

He couldn't seem to squelch his amusement. "I'm sure you do."

"Well, my dad agreed to a courtship between us, didn't he?"

"You have a point."

"I'm praying about other things too."

"Like what?"

"You and your Amish grandparents."

"Don't even bother. That's a lost cause."

"Why do you hate your grandparents so much?"

"I don't *hate* them." He sighed.

"You say that, but I don't know how truthful it is. Your words and actions prove otherwise."

In that moment, his face transformed. His eyes flashed with something akin to fury, similar to what she'd seen during their Walmart excursion, but this look seemed to convey sadness as well.

She dared to lightly touched his forearm. "Will you share what you're thinking with me?"

He worked his jaw and swallowed. "I don't know if I can."

"Please?" She glanced up to see if others in the fellowship hall could hear their conversation. They occupied a table toward the back corner of the large room, so it was unlikely. No one seemed to be paying them any heed.

"I don't remember too much. I was young, maybe Jaycee's age." He blew out a noisy breath and clenched his hands. "Mom had spent the better part of the morning baking, since Dad had said his folks loved baked goods. She was excited to finally get the opportunity to meet Dad's parents for the first time."

"You had never met them then?"

"No. I don't think I knew they even existed. It was different with Grandma and Grandpa Mills, Mom's parents. They were like normal grandparents, even though they lived in a different state and we didn't see them all that often. But I was excited when I found out about Dad's parents because I thought, you know, Wesley and I would get another set of grandparents. And they didn't even live that far away from us." He shook his head and his frown deepened.

"Boy, was I wrong. We pulled up to their house and we all got out of the car. I still remember Wesley teasing me about us getting spoiled since we were their only grandchildren. Anyway, when Dad went and knocked on the door, my grandmother answered. She'd smiled, but it wasn't like I'd expected. Mom handed the baked goods to her, but she didn't take them. Then my grandfather came up behind her. I couldn't understand the words he exchanged with Dad because they weren't speaking English, but I knew by the tone it wasn't a pleasant conversation. Dad told us all to go get into the car. I didn't understand why.

"He and my grandpa argued with each other for the next several minutes. Mom cried the whole way home, all the goodies she baked still in her arms. Wesley and I cried too. We wouldn't even eat the treats. I think we were just so disheartened with how the events played out, we'd lost our appetites. And the treats reminded us of our grandparents' rejection. They didn't care about us, or if we even existed, it seemed. It crushed me. It crushed us all. Dad hadn't said more than a few words to any of us for the next week or so. I think he just had to process it in his own way. They must've told him to never come back. Because we never did."

Randy shoved away tears with his fists. "I'm sorry."

Tears pricked Holly's eyes too. "No, don't apologize. You were hurt deeply."

"I've never shared that with anyone before."

She reached over and squeezed his hand. "Thank you for confiding in me. It means a lot."

"I didn't mean to dump all my emotional baggage on you."

"The load is lighter when more people carry it, right?"

"Thank you for listening." He shrugged. "Although, I don't know what good it did to tell you."

"It helps me understand you better. And, in some small way, I think it helps you to talk about it."

"It doesn't matter."

"I think it does. It has defined who you are." She frowned, attempting to process everything he'd just said. "But what I don't understand is…your grandfather *talked* to you in Walmart…did something change?"

"Two years ago my grandparents started coming around."

She remembered Shannon mentioning it, but she wanted Randy's point of view. "Around?"

"They visited the last two Christmases, and they've visited with my parents a few times."

"So you guys are no longer shunned, then?"

He shrugged. "I guess *we* never were. It was my dad who was shunned."

"But they refused the baked goods. And they wouldn't see you."

"I know. I don't know their reasons for that. But according to my dad, they don't have a problem with the rest of us, only him because he'd been baptized into the Amish church before he left."

"I'm confused. Why would they visit your parents if your dad is shunned?"

"Honestly, I think they've been visiting in secret. Their church doesn't know."

"Oh." Shannon had said something similar, hadn't she?

"Like I said. It's just dumb religious rules. Things that men made up."

"Do you know what the word 'religion' means?"

"Not specifically, but I think I have a pretty good idea."

"Well, it probably has more than one meaning. But the book of James says, *Pure religion and undefiled before God and the Father is this, to visit the fatherless and widows in their affliction, and to keep himself unspotted from the world.*"

"I don't know if I see your point."

"My point is that you probably shouldn't lump everything 'religious' together. Religion in itself isn't stupid or dumb. Now, if you're talking about *false religion*, I totally agree with you. False religion keeps people *from* God."

"I guess I'm talking about false religion, then."

"Not even Jesus got along with the religious leaders of His day, although He attempted to open their eyes to the Truth. Christianity is totally different than a bunch of religious rules."

He nodded.

"Have you ever talked to your grandparents about it? Gotten their perspective?"

His frown deepened. "Why would I want to do that?"

She rubbed her forehead. "Randy." She had to remind herself to be patient with him.

"What?"

"Look, I'm not saying they're right. I just think it would help you to see this through their eyes."

"What good would it do?" He shook his head. "Listen, Holly, I know you're trying to help. But sitting down with my grandparents? Just, no."

For crying out loud, this man was stubborn. "Why not?"

"I don't want to."

"So, you'd rather hold on to your bitterness and anger for the rest of your life?"

Randy squeezed his eyes close.

She tried to speak gently. "Wouldn't you rather deal with this and put it behind you?"

"I just don't think talking about it is going to help anything."

"But you don't *know* that."

He rubbed his temples. "Why are you doing this? Why do you care?"

"I thought it was obvious."

"It isn't."

"I like you. A lot. I want to see you happy."

"I'm happy around you."

She frowned. "You look miserable right now."

"You know what I mean. Not when we're discussing my grandparents."

"See, that's the thing, Randy. You can't just bury your past hurts. They don't just go away. They poison you from the inside out. They affect your relationships with those around you. If we are to have a healthy relationship—or any relationship at all—you need to learn to deal with things like this. Because there will eventually be something else that offends you in the future."

"Listen, I already know their side of the story. I've talked to Wesley about it."

"And what does he say?"

"He doesn't agree with their position either."

"So, he doesn't get along with your grandparents?" She already knew the answer.

"He gets along great with them."

"So…why can't you?"

"It's complicated."

"It doesn't have to be. If Wesley's found a way to bridge that relationship, can't you?"

He clenched his hands. "I'm not Wesley. And I never will be."

"Randy." She sighed. "I know you're not Wesley. And I don't *want* you to be."

"Really? That's not what it seems like to me."

"You're changing the subject."

"Maybe because I don't want to talk about this." He turned away from her.

She blew out a breath. "Fine."

His head snapped back and he examined her. "Fine? Really?"

"Well, I'm obviously getting nowhere, so I'm not going to waste my breath anymore." What was the point? He'd definitely need to work through his bullheadedness. It could be a good trait if channeled properly, but right now, he was going down the wrong channel.

He lifted his hands in exasperation. "Fine, I'll talk to my grandparents!"

She blinked. Had she heard him right? "You will?"

"On one condition."

She raised a brow, staring at the digit he pointed upward.

His gaze zeroed in on hers. "*You* come with me."

She smiled now. "I'd be happy to."

"You would?"

She nodded.

He reached over and squeezed her hand, but just for a second. "Good."

"But we'd need to take someone else with us," Holly said as they both stood from the table.

"I can go!"

Holly and Randy both jumped, their mouths agape, staring down at Jaycee, who had sprung up from under the table.

"Jaycee!" Randy frowned. "How long have you been under there?"

"A lo-o-o-ng time. You guys talk *forever*." Randy's young brother-in-law/nephew rolled his eyes.

Holly giggled.

"Jaycee!" Wesley rushed up to them. "There you are! We've been looking for you all over the place. Your sister wants to go home."

"Shannon *always* wants to go home." He sighed dramatically, then turning his attention to Randy, bounced up and down on his tiptoes. "Can I go? Can I go?"

Wesley frowned and glanced back and forth from Randy to Holly. "Go where?"

"It turns out Jaycee here has been hiding under our table during our conversation, probably eavesdropping the entire time." Randy eyed him in disapproval, but Holly found him hilarious. Jaycee was one of the students in her Sunday school class and he never ceased to make her smile. Although, she would admit, he could be a little exasperating at times as well.

"It wasn't my fault. Really, it wasn't. I was hiding from Bright. How was I to know that Randy and his sweetheart would come and sit here and talk *for-ev-er*? And I wasn't dropping no eaves, neither. Besides, all Randy wants to talk about is how cute his girlfriend is…blah." Jaycee pointed his finger in his mouth as though to gag himself.

Holly had to press her lips together.

"And they talked about Santa and *Mammi*." Jaycee scratched his head. "I didn't know they was mean to you and Randy and Grandma and Grandpa Stoltz."

Wesley frowned at Randy.

Randy sighed and shook his head. "I'm sorry. The conversation was meant for Holly's ears, not mischievous little boys." He ruffled Jaycee's hair.

"I'm sorry." Jaycee overdramatized his pouty lip, as he seemed to do with everything.

Wesley cocked his head, looking at Jaycee. "Are you really?"

"For sure and for certain." His serious head bobbed up and down.

Wesley eyed Randy and Holly. "So, is he forgiven?"

Randy's lips twitched as his gaze met Holly's. "I don't know…" Randy sighed loudly and dramatically shook his head. "He might have to volunteer for some chaperone time."

"What's trombone time mean?" Jaycee's lips twisted.

Holly couldn't hold in her laugh this time.

"Chaperone time, buddy," Wesley said. "It means you might have to go somewhere with Uncle Randy and Miss Holly."

"To Santa's?" He jumped up and down. "For reals?"

"I don't know…" Wesley raised a brow. "That might just be a reward."

"You know, you're probably right." Randy shot his brother a mischievous wink. "We should have Brighton go along instead."

"Aww…" Jaycee's bottom lip stuck out at least half an inch. "I said I was sorry. I'll never drop eaves again. Promise." His pointing finger made a crossing motion over his heart.

Holly glanced at Randy. "Drop eaves?"

"It's a reference to the movie *Lord of the Rings*. You haven't seen it?"

She shook her head.

"It's *really* scary," Jaycee chimed in.

Her hand flew to her heart. "Oh. I don't think I'd want to see it, then."

"It's super cool, though," Jaycee added, his eyes wide.

Randy chuckled. "I'm not sure Holly enjoys those kinds of movies."

Jaycee's face scrunched up. "Do you like the kissing ones, like Shannon?"

Holly glanced at Wesley for clarification.

"Hallmark." He shrugged.

She turned to Jaycee and smiled. "Yes, I do enjoy those once in a while."

"Take notes, brother." Wesley squeezed Randy's shoulder. He then tousled Jaycee's hair. "Time to scoot, young man. Shannon's probably waiting in the car with the little ones."

After saying their goodbyes to Wesley and Jaycee, Holly and Randy moved toward the main auditorium.

"Your family is probably wanting to leave too," Randy said.

"You're likely right."

"Will your parents be cool with Jaycee going along or would they prefer another adult?"

"I think Jaycee will be fine, but maybe we should take Brighton along too so they can keep each other occupied. That way, we can have a chance to speak openly with your grandparents." She surveyed Randy's countenance, guessing there were gritted teeth behind his forced smile.

"Yeah." He blew out a breath.

"I'm free tomorrow. Maybe after the kids get out of school?"

"Tomorrow?"

She heard the hesitancy in his tone. He held the door open for her to exit.

"Better to get it over with, right?" She attempted a reassuring smile. They were in this together.

"I guess so. I'll talk to Wesley to see if the kids will be able to go then." He smiled. "Wow. It seems like I've gotten to see you every day this week. How lucky can a man get?" He winked, sending her heart aflutter.

TWELVE

Randy checked his phone again, just to make sure Holly hadn't called to cancel. The fresh powdering of snow they'd received overnight, and then again this afternoon, would have been a good excuse. If he were going with anyone but Holly, he would have taken the opportunity to jump ship. If he were going with anyone but Holly, he would have said no. If he were going with anyone but Holly, the burst of confidence he felt would be non-existent.

Confidence aside, he still didn't want to do this. But he would. For Holly.

At least the road crews were great at keeping the snow off the streets, he mused before turning into Wesley's driveway.

The boys had been ready to go and sprinted to his vehicle the moment he pulled up. His lips twisted as he surveyed their bosoms, overflowing with snow toys.

Randy frowned. "What's this all about?"

"Wesley said we could," Jaycee insisted, setting a plastic sled down at his feet.

"They have a pretty sweet hill on their property. It's perfect for tubing." Brighton held up a black inner tube with one arm, a snowboard was in his other.

"And they have a pond. I brought my ice skates!" Jaycee beamed.

Randy couldn't blame him for being excited about ice skating.

"Okay. I'll pop the trunk." Randy shook his head. Just how long did these boys think they'd be staying? His idea had been to get in, say what needed to be said, then get out. As soon as possible.

Wesley and Shannon both waved from the porch, as the kids entered his vehicle. "Have fun!" Wesley called out.

"Yeah. Fun." Randy mumbled under his breath, then turned the engine over.

"We always have lots of fun at *Mammi* and Santa's." Jaycee bounced on the backseat.

That boy had more energy than anyone Randy had ever seen.

"Wow! Look at all the snow!" Jaycee exclaimed as they headed toward the Remington residence.

Apparently, Jaycee and Brighton hadn't been the

only ones with fun in mind today. Near several houses they'd passed, children of all ages had been outside taking full advantage of the powdery white stuff.

"Did you two bring your hat and gloves?"

"Of course." Brighton rolled his eyes. "Shannon won't let us step a foot outside without them. She acts like we're three."

Randy grinned. "That's what mothers do."

"Yeah, but she's our sister."

Randy glanced into the rearview mirror. "Maybe so. But she's also a mom to you now, or at least your authority. When your parents passed away, the courts gave her guardianship. That means you should honor and respect her because she's the adult in charge."

"You sound just like Wesley," Jaycee mumbled.

"I do?" Randy smiled to himself. *Good.*

He pulled up to a lovely white Victorian two-story home. Pine bunting, with bright red bows at each interval, lined the spacious porch. The classic wicker furniture on one side of the porch and cozy wooden swing on the other invited him to come, sit, and enjoy a glass of sweet tea. Well, it would in summertime, anyway. Right now, wassail or hot cocoa would be in order.

Randy smiled at the thought of cuddling with Holly on the porch—hot cocoa in their hands, a cozy blanket wrapped around the two of them, while their lips meshed together in sweet bliss. He shook himself from his daydream. That was something that would likely never happen, at least, not this side of the marriage altar.

The marriage altar? Yeah, that was still a long way off. It would be better to lock those thoughts away, lest he act on them and be banished from the Remington home permanently.

"Wow! That looks like those houses in some of the movies Shannon likes to watch!"

Indeed.

Holly scurried down the steps, looking gorgeous as ever. Her brown curls peeked out from the sides of the beanie she wore, her cheeks alive with color, making her even more irresistible. How on earth was he ever going to refrain from touching her? Especially when all he wanted to do was take her into his arms and hold her close. It seemed like she became more attractive to him every time he saw her. How was that possible?

He jumped out and opened the door for her. Her smile warmed him from the inside out.

"You ready to do this?" Her eyes sparkled.

He grunted. "No. But I have a feeling it will be worth it, just because I get to spend time with you."

Her cheeks flushed at his words.

He hurried back to his side of the car and hopped in.

"Can we go on the roller coaster road?" Jaycee leaned forward, poking his head between Randy and Holly.

"Roller coaster road?" Holly's brow rose.

"The eight hundred." Randy shook his head. "Sorry, buddy. It's out of the way."

"Please. Please. Please." Jaycee urged.

Randy looked at Holly. "Do you mind? I don't think we can dissuade him."

"It sounds like fun to me." She shrugged.

"Okay, the roller coaster road it is."

"Yes!" Jaycee pumped a fist into the air.

As Randy turned onto the "roller coaster road" as Jaycee called it, she immediately noticed the road signs indicating there were Amish buggies in the area.

"I didn't realize there were Amish down this road."

"Have you ever been this way?" Randy glanced at her.

She nodded. "I have, but not in forever."

"We come on this road *all* the time!" Jaycee leaned forward joining in the conversation.

"Not *all* the time, Jaycee," Brighton added his two cents.

"Let's stop at Millers' and bring *Mammi* and Santa a pot pie!" Jaycee's grin widened.

"You just want Uncle Randy to buy you a cinnamon roll," Brighton challenged.

"Do not." Jaycee gave an exaggerated shake of his head. "*Mammi* will have cookies for us. Shan said I couldn't eat too many."

Holly chuckled.

"Do you want to stop?" Randy eyed her as he slowed down in front of the small store.

She shrugged. "Sure." But she wondered if Randy wasn't indulging Jaycee's every whim in order to stall their visit to his grandparents' house.

Snow crunched under the tires as Randy pulled into the long driveway and stopped next to a small building that was Millers' Country Store and Bakery. He hurried around to open the door for her.

"Thank you." She smiled up at him as he offered his hand to help her out of the car. He held it longer than necessary, but she didn't mind one bit. Being with Randy made her want to break all the rules. And that was *not* a good thing.

She felt his hand on the small of her back as they walked into the little store. Randy didn't seem to comprehend her father's idea of "no touching." *Her father's idea?* No, it was something she'd assented to as well. She just never thought it would be *this* hard to keep her boundaries in place. Not when she dreamt of Randy's kisses the moment her head hit the pillow at night. And often in her daydreams as well, in spite of herself.

A war definitely waged within.

Holly had to remind herself that physical attraction was one thing and love was another. She couldn't get the two confused. She refused to settle for a relationship built on physical attraction alone. She'd already seen too much of that in her friends' marriages, which were now in shambles. She wanted something genuine and lasting. She wanted a man to love her for who she was, not for her looks. She wanted what Shannon and Wesley had. What her parents had.

"Should we get one or two?" Randy's words forced her mind to snap back to reality.

She surveyed the pot pies behind the glass enclosure in front of them. "Just in case they want us to stay and share it with them, we'd better get two."

Randy's lips pursed together. Probably because she'd mentioned staying and sharing a meal with his Amish grandparents.

"You've got this," she gently reminded him.

He blew out a breath. "Yeah. Sure." The anxiety written on Randy's face made her ponder whether people could experience emotional PTSD from childhood memories. She'd have to look it up later.

"We'll take two of the pot pies," he told the Amish woman behind the counter.

"Anything else?" the woman asked.

Randy's gaze flitted to the two boys, who looked longingly at the cinnamon rolls. "We'll take four cinnamon rolls as well."

The woman rang up the total and Randy paid for their items. She handed them two bags. "Thank you."

As they walked out and made their way back to the vehicle, Jaycee insisted on sounding every single windchime hanging from the porch.

"Let's go, Jaycee," Randy called.

"Do we get to eat our cinnamon rolls right now?" Jaycee's smile widened as he slid into the car and buckled himself in.

"Who said one of those is for you?" Randy teased.

"'Cause you always get us one when we drive by here."

Randy glanced into the rearview mirror, putting a finger to his lips. "Just don't tell Wesley that or he'll have me contributing to your dental bill."

"He already knows," Jaycee divulged.

"In that case, maybe I'll get you a toothbrush and toothpaste for Christmas." Randy grinned.

"Nah. Grandma and Grandpa already get us those in our stocking every year."

Randy chuckled. "That doesn't surprise me."

About ten minutes later, they pulled into the driveway of an Amish farm. Holly's eyes immediately went to the black Amish buggy, then moved to the plain white two-story house. Did his grandparents live in this large house all alone?

She noticed laundry hanging on the line, flapping in what little frigid wind they had. Did clothing still dry in freezing cold temperatures? Another thing she'd have to look up online.

"Wesley always parks in back," Brighton informed them.

"Well, I'm not Wesley," Randy growled.

"It's so the church people don't know he's visiting," Jaycee shared.

"We'll park here," Randy insisted defiantly. He closed his eyes.

Holly glanced at him, noting his clenched jaw. Was he remembering the last time he'd come here with his family? She reached over and briefly placed her hand over his. "I'm praying for you."

"Yeah, thanks." He drew in a deep breath.

Before they knew it, Jaycee and Brighton had hopped out of Randy's car and raced to the front door.

The door opened, and "Santa" as Jaycee had called him, ushered the two boys inside. The older Amish man stood sentry just outside the door, his gaze focused on their vehicle.

"Should we go in?" Holly suggested.

"I guess." He swallowed. "This is harder than I thought."

"I know." She squeezed his hand. "But God is with you, and He'll help you."

She glanced at the floorboard. "Do you want me to carry in the pot pies?"

"No. I think it's better if I have something in my hands."

She passed the bag to him.

"We'll leave the cinnamon rolls here. I might need a consolation prize when our visit is over," he mumbled.

Please show me how I can help Randy, Lord. And please let this visit go well.

THIRTEEN

You can do this. Randy attempted to give himself a pep talk, but with each laden step closer to his Amish grandfather, his anxiety seemed to escalate. It wasn't until Holly reached for his hand that he realized he'd stopped walking all together.

Holly moved to stand directly in front of him and met him with a steady gaze. "Randy…" She dared to touch his cheek, something he was certain was *not* in her courtship rule book. "Let's just get this over with, okay? We don't have to stay long if you don't want to." She'd kept her voice low.

"I don't know what to say," he quietly admitted.

"Then don't say anything. Just nod a greeting and we'll go inside," she whispered.

"Alright." He expelled a frosty breath, and they continued toward the porch.

"I never thought I'd see the day my youngest *gross*

sohn would enter my home," his grandfather said, holding the door open for him and Holly.

He simply nodded. Because if he said what was on his mind, he'd likely ruin this visit. If he said what was on his mind, they'd be heading out the driveway as quickly as they'd driven in. If he said what was on his mind, this amazing woman at his side would probably dump him like yesterday's garbage.

His grandfather closed the door behind them, then turned to Holly. "And you are?"

"I'm Holly." She smiled and held out a friendly hand in greeting.

"Christopher." He took her hand, his gaze flicking to Randy.

"Nice to meet you, Christopher," she added.

His grandmother walked into the entryway, surprise brightening her face.

"It's our youngest *gross sohn*." His grandfather smiled tentatively at Randy's grandmother.

"I see that." She didn't hesitate to move close, examine Randy, then engulf him in a hug. "It's so *gut* to see you. You look just like your father did when he was a *youngie*."

"Doesn't he?" His grandfather said, placing a hand on Randy's upper arm.

Randy resisted the urge to shake it off. Although

he'd had limited contact with them the last two Christmases, these people were virtually strangers to him. He felt no emotional ties to them whatsoever. And that had suited him well thus far.

Jaycee bounded into the room. "*Mammi* has cookies!"

"*Jah, kumm*. Have some cookies," his grandmother urged, leading the way to the kitchen.

Arching a brow, Holly glanced at Randy. She nodded toward the kitchen.

He grunted inwardly, but followed his grandmother as Holly suggested. He stared down at the plastic bag dangling from his arm. Holly noticed and nudged him.

Did she have any idea what she was asking of him? How could she expect him to offer a gift to people he'd been angry with the majority of his life? He looked at her and shook his head. His lips seemed to seal shut. He couldn't force the words out of his mouth.

"Randy stopped by the Millers' store and bought some pot pies for you," Holly said, prompting him with an encouraging smile.

She had said the necessary words, but it seemed she was determined to make *him* offer the gifts he held in his hand. Instead, he set the bag on the table.

His grandmother peeked inside. "Oh, those look *wunderbaar*! Ain't so, Christopher?" She pulled them out of the bag.

"From Millers', you say?" His grandfather directed the question at Randy.

He gave a nod, his mouth refusing to operate.

"Kayla Miller makes the best pot pies." His grandmother beamed. "This is a special treat. *Denki*. Thank you."

"It was his pleasure," Holly insisted.

His mouth agape, he stared at Holly. Had she just told a bold-faced lie? She knew good and well he was dreading every minute of this. As a matter of fact, if it weren't for Holly, he wouldn't even be here.

"Santa, can Bright and me go see the puppies? Please, please, please?" Jaycee's plea broke through the awkwardness.

His grandfather chuckled. "That's fine by me. *Chust* have a care around the horses."

"We will. C'mon, Bright!" Jaycee charged toward the door.

"Put your coat and gloves on," Randy called. "Your sister will have my hide if I let you go out in the cold without them."

"Shannon is quite protective of her siblings," his grandmother said. "Well, now, should we dish out some of this delightful treat?"

"I'd love some." Holly smiled. "Randy?"

"Yeah. Sure." He swallowed.

This all felt so strange, like he was in a dream. He lifted his head and let his eyes wander the surroundings. It seemed quite dark in the dining area, likely due to the abundance of dark wood and absence of electric lights. A lone lantern flickered in the middle of the table, and natural light filtered in through the blue-curtain clad windows.

It occurred to him that this was his first time inside an Amish home—a place he *should* have...*would* have visited many times in his twenty-one years, if his family had been welcomed.

"Why the welcome now?" He blurted aloud.

All eyes turned to him and warmth rose up his neck.

"What was that, *sohn*?" His grandfather's bushy eyebrow hitched upward.

"Why are you welcoming us into your home *now*, when you rejected our family and sent us away all those years ago?" His fist clenched tight.

He knew Holly's gaze bored into him. He hadn't looked at her, but he could somehow feel it.

He pinned a stare on his grandfather and grandmother, requesting—no *demanding*—truth.

"Your *vatter* was in the *bann*." His grandmother's words were whispered.

He lifted a hand of empty air. "That means absolutely nothing to me."

"Randy…" Holly's voice quietly urged him to be civil.

"I don't understand how you so readily took in Shannon and the kids, but you showed nothing but disdain for your own son and his family," he challenged.

"You don't understand our ways," his grandfather said.

"Your ways suck."

Holly gasped. "Randy."

"It comes from the Bible." Had his grandfather *really* just said that?

"No." Randy shook his head. "Don't tell me that's what Jesus would do, because it isn't. He said. "Let the little children come to me, and hinder them not." So, tell me, was he just talking about strangers' children, or *all* children—even your own grandchildren?"

"We were wrong about that part," his grandfather admitted. "But that is not where the *bann* comes from. When someone turns away from the faith, we are supposed to shun them and pray for them until they come back to the fold."

"I don't claim to know a ton about that Bible, but if you're referring to the passage in Corinthians about the man taking his father's wife, this is *hardly* the same thing."

"We refer to the end of the chapter where it is

written not to have fellowship with a brother who has gone the wrong way and refuses to repent. When your father took the kneeling vow in baptism, he agreed to abide by and uphold the rules of the Amish church. This vow, like the marriage vow, was only to be broken by death. Nobody forced your father to take the vow in his youth. It was his own decision."

"See, that's another thing I don't get. You say that it was his own decision, but was it really? He said he wouldn't have been allowed to date unless he joined the church. That sounds an awful lot like manipulation to me."

"How can a man lead a wife and family if he himself is not committed to *Gott*? A commitment to *Der Herr* and the church must come first or else the house will fall, *sohn*. Do you not believe this?"

Randy's jaw slacked, and his gaze moved to Holly. Hadn't he just had a similar discussion with Holly's father? "Yeah. I guess I agree with that part."

"Randy." His grandfather stopped talking until Randy's eyes met his. "Your *grossmammi* and I were wrong to turn your family away that day. We have regretted it many times over the years. We want to ask for your forgiveness. We cannot do anything about the past, but we can have a relationship that begins now. And we would very much like to have that with you, as we do with your brother."

Randy's lips tightened and pressed together.

His grandmother joined his grandfather and he took her hand in his. They both stood before Randy. "Will you forgive us?"

He suddenly felt a warm delicate hand on his shoulder, and glanced up to see Holly. When had she vacated her seat at the table and gone to stand behind him?

Randy closed his eyes and swallowed. Moments ticked by in silence as he wrestled with his thoughts and emotions. How could he just forgive and forget the past? The years of feeling rejected. The years of feeling unwanted. The years of feeling unworthy of their love.

"We know now that *Gott* would have us reconcile, even if it is not in the way we'd hoped or imagined. We see that He is giving us a second chance before our time on this earth is over. But *you* have to be willing as well. We will not make you. *Nee*, forgiveness is not something that can be forced. It must come from the heart."

His grandfather's words pierced through his soul, like an arrow severing his skin and sinking deep into his heart. Randy's head dropped into his hands and he cursed the moisture gathering on his lashes. His heart clenched tightly and a sob escaped his lips unbidden. He couldn't speak if he tried.

And then, like a whirlwind, he was standing on his feet, ingulfed in his grandfather's arms. His grandmother then joined them, and pulled Holly into their circle of love as well.

"I forgive you," he managed to say as he broke away. But he suspected that if he'd said nothing at all, his grandparents would have understood. He couldn't honestly say that he felt it fully, but a dam inside him had broken, and healing had begun.

Commotion at the door stole their attention.

"*Dawdi*, someone just pulled up in a buggy." Brighton sounded out of breath, like he'd run to the house.

Holly eyed Randy and nodded. "We should probably go now."

His grandparents didn't argue with her words. As if they'd rather have their church people there than them. *Stop it.* He condemned his accusatory thoughts.

"I'll get Jaycee." Brighton rushed back out.

"You will come back again soon then?" his grandmother asked, hopefulness in her tone.

Randy nodded.

"Let me pack some goodies for you." His grandmother began moving about the kitchen.

"Excuse me." His grandfather's look was apologetic. "I must see who has come." He shoved his coat and hat on, then disappeared out the door.

"Aww…" Jaycee's voice sounded through the house. "Do we have to leave *already*?"

"I'm afraid so, bud." Randy grimaced at his nephew.

"But me and Bright haven't even gone sledding yet," he protested.

"Another time maybe."

"Aww…"

"I know. But they have Amish company now, so we need to scoot." He squeezed Jaycee's shoulder. "Say goodbye, then go get into the car."

"Okay," he mumbled. His chin hung to his chest as his sluggish feet plunked toward the kitchen.

Randy chuckled to himself. The kid had more theatrics in him than The Center for the Performing Arts.

Randy walked back toward the kitchen to see if Holly was ready to go. His grandmother handed her back the two bags they'd brought, but they looked to be filled with different items. His grandmother moved to him and took his hand in hers. Tears shimmered in her eyes. "Thank you for coming today. You don't know how much this means to your grandfather and me."

He swallowed and nodded. "Thank you." It was all he could manage.

He glanced at Holly. Was that a look of admiration in her eyes?

As they ambled toward the car, Holly bumped his arm and smiled. He opened the door for her, but she hesitated, staring into his eyes. He had to refrain from dipping his head and stealing a kiss.

"What?" He couldn't resist reaching up and letting her soft hair slide through his fingers.

"I'm so proud of you."

Her words warmed him from the inside out. *God, this woman is perfect for me.* "Thank you for saying that."

She briefly squeezed his hand, then slid into the car.

This day hadn't gone so bad after all.

FOURTEEN

"Bye, Santa!" Young Jaycee threw his arms around Christopher's middle, nearly knocking him off his feet.

Christopher chuckled and patted the boy's back, even though Henry, the district deacon, wore a disapproving look. But Christopher wouldn't begrudge his honorary grandson's affection, neither would he reject it. He had enough mistakes to live with as it was.

"Did your *grossmammi* give you some cookies to take home?" He smiled down at the boy.

"Yes, she did!" He bounced on his toes. "And I'm going to eat them *all* before I get home, otherwise Shan will only let me have one."

He chuckled again. He didn't doubt this boy could brighten up anyone's day. Jaycee did Christopher's heart good.

"You best be going now. It looks like your *onkel* is

already getting into the car."

"Okay. See ya!" The boy spun around and disappeared as quickly as he'd come.

"*Ach*, to have that kind of energy again," Christopher mused aloud as he watched the vehicle exiting the driveway.

"Back to the matter at hand," the deacon not-so-gently reminded him.

Christopher's smile faded. "I only have so much time left on this earth."

"And you choose to spend it in disobedience to the *Ordnung*?" Minister Reuben interjected.

"*Nee*. I intend to spend it in obedience to Christ. I cannot deny what my conscience is proclaiming inside my head and heart."

"And what's that?"

He eyed the three men, hoping *Der Herr* would use him to speak to their hearts. "Christ dwelt with common people, not the religious crowd. He commanded us to love one another as He loved us. This *Meidung*, what we've been doing, is not showing God's love. Jesus showed us what that looked like. He ate with sinners. He touched the lepers. He had compassion on the weak. He loved those shunned by the religious leaders. Remember the man blind from birth?"

The men nodded. "*Jah*, but that's not—"

He couldn't help his voice rising. "The religious leaders kicked him out of the synagogue for following Jesus. If the same fate happens to me, then so be it."

"You know well enough what this *g'may* believed and practiced when you joined. You took vows in agreement. Will you go back on that now? Will you follow in your *Englisch sohn's* footsteps?"

"Should a man continue down a path that he knows leads to destruction?" Christopher challenged.

The deacon's arms crossed over his chest and his lips pursed tightly.

Minister Graber frowned. "Are you saying our ways lead to destruction?"

"*Nee.* And *jah.* I've seen the destruction that adherence to *some* of our ways has caused my family. My own *gross sohn*, whom I'd only seen once briefly during his childhood, hated me. We must consider who our actions or inactions affect. Who am I to incite hate in another human being?"

"The hatred was his own choice."

"He was a *kind*! All he knew was what he saw—what had transpired between myself and *mei sohn*. And I assure you he did *not* see love in the ways of our people." Christopher shook his head. "Oh, I thought it was love at the time. But I was wrong. So terribly wrong. I see that now."

"You are the bishop! The leader of our people. You must set an example of obedience or you know what will happen. The *Englisch* ways will start creeping into the *g'may* and before we know it, there will be no difference between us and *der velt*. We *cannot* have that."

"What about Judah Hostettler's district?"

"The bishop in Pennsylvania?" The deacon scoffed. "They're hardly even Amish!"

"They drive horse and buggy and dress Plain just like us."

"*Jah*, but that's about it. The things he allows in his *g'may* are scandalous."

"You are wrong. Do you know what I, all those in *his* congregation, and those who know him best see? We see love. We see grace. His heart is good. He desires the will of *Der Herr*. Are his people perfect? *Nee*. But neither are we. He leads with wisdom and he is the closest man to Jesus I've ever known. Ask Bishop Bontrager in Rexville. He'll tell you the same thing."

The deacon snorted. "Jerry Bontrager? Another shepherd who can't seem to keep his flock inside the fence."

"So it's pride that keeps us from the love of Jesus, then." Christopher knew he shouldn't have said that, but this conversation was getting ridiculous.

"*Nee*. It is *not* pride! We are to keep ourselves unspotted from the world."

"We can do that and *still* show love. Don't you see? That is what Jesus did." *Father, please open their hearts.* "My son may drive a truck and dress *Englisch*, but he is a good, Godly man. He loves his family. He walks uprightly. He attends church faithfully. He does not live a wicked lifestyle."

"But he was born Amish. He was baptized Amish."

"I realize that. Again, I ask you. Should a man continue down a path that he knows leads to destruction?" He eyed the men carefully. "I know *Der Herr* chose me for this position, and I do not take it lightly. I love *most* of the ways of our people. But when we see that something is not working, maybe we need to consider changing it. I realize we don't like change. But sometimes Gott opens our eyes and shows us a better way. Some changes are for the better. I can't help but think that perhaps *Der Herr* has put me here for such a time as this."

"We have already discussed this privately, and we've made our decision. Since you will not submit to the *Ordnung*, you are to be placed under the *bann*."

Christopher's heart ached deeply. Not because they'd placed him under the *bann*, but because his people, these ones he loved and lived amongst, were rejecting the ways of *Gott*. A song popped into his head and he couldn't help but utter the words aloud. "Though none go with me, still I will follow."

Later, Christopher and his *fraa,* Judy, sat in the main room, enjoying the warmth of the fire as a brisk breeze picked up out yonder.

"You will not consider becoming an *Englischer* and driving a car, will you? Seventy-five is too old to be learning *Englisch* ways, I'm thinking." Judy's knitting needles clacked together in rhythm.

Christopher grinned. "A car, you say? I hadn't thought of that. I think I still might remember how to drive from my *youngie* days."

Judy gasped. Her knitting needles stilled. "You never told me you had a car!"

Christopher chuckled. "That's because I knew you probably wouldn't have let me court you if you thought I was one of those worldly boys."

She nodded. "You're right. I probably wouldn't."

"*Ach*, the things we needlessly worry over. Do you really think *Der Herr* cares whether we drive a car or a horse and buggy?"

"*Nee*. He cares about the heart." She continued her

project. No doubt, a Christmas gift for one of the *kinskinner*. He knew better than to ask. His *fraa* pinned him with a gaze, her mien sober. "So what will you do now?"

"I will follow where *Der Herr* leads me. I will follow what I know the Scriptures are telling me. I will follow in the footsteps of Jesus."

"That sounds like a *gut* plan, husband. And I will follow you." A smile brightened her face.

Christopher reached over and squeezed her hand, his eyes misting with tears. In all of their trials, he still considered himself one of the most blessed men that ever walked the face of the earth.

FIFTEEN

"We weren't there as long as I thought we'd be. It's still early. Do you want to come over?" Randy's brow rose as he tapped his fingers on the steering wheel. "My parents are home."

More time with this handsome man she'd been quickly falling in love with? Yes, please.

"What about the boys?"

"I'm sure they'd love to spend a little time with Grandma and Grandpa."

"We would! We would!" Jaycee bounced up and down in the back seat.

Holly loved Jaycee's enthusiasm.

"But no peeking under the tree." Randy eyed the two boys in the rearview mirror.

"Aw, what's the fun in that?" Brighton protested.

"I'm sure there will be something for you to do," Randy said.

"Grandma will probably make us wrap presents like last time." Jaycee's fervor deflated.

"Oh, I love wrapping presents!" Holly smiled.

"Yeah, but it's no fun if you don't get to see what's in 'em," Jaycee mumbled.

"Oh, I think that makes it even *more* fun," Holly insisted.

"How so?"

"Well, because then it's like a mystery. You feel it to try to see if you can figure it out that way. Or you shake it to see if you can hear any clues. If that doesn't work, then you smell it."

"You smell it?" Jaycee's nose scrunched up.

"Could be chocolate." She nodded. "Or something even more cool. One time, my brother figured out he was getting a gun just by smelling the box."

"Really?" Jaycee's eyes widened and he turned to Brighton. "That's super cool!"

"How'd he know that?" Brighton scratched his head, his lips twisted in puzzlement.

Holly giggled mischievously. "Well, the box *was* the size of a hunting rifle."

"That's not smelling!"

Holly shrugged. "At the time, I believed him. I think I was five."

"Five-year-olds don't know nothing." Jaycee waved a dismissive hand.

"You mean they think old Amish guys are Santa Claus." Brighton laughed and poked his younger brother in the side.

"Hey, *Dawdi* Christopher *did* look like Santa!"

Holly's head tilted. "I can see that."

"See?" Jaycee's arms crossed over his chest and he dismissed Brighton's comment with a nod. "Miss Holly says so, and she's really smart."

"She sure is." Randy shot her a wink. "Even though she's letting me court her. But we won't hold that against her."

"I think you're fun, Uncle Randy," Brighton said. "Why wouldn't Miss Holly like you?"

"Yeah. You took us on the roller coaster road and bought us cinnamon rolls!" Jaycee grinned.

He glanced at his nephew in the rearview mirror. "Doesn't Wesley take you on that road too?"

"He does, but it's no fun anymore. Not like with you. Shan doesn't like for him to drive fast on the hills no more." Jaycee's lower lip protruded. "Not since she had the *boppli*."

Holly's brow rose and she glanced at Randy for clarification. "*Boppli*?"

"It's 'baby' in Amish," Brighton explained.

"That's what *Mammi* calls Olivia and Melanie," Jaycee added.

"*Boppli*." Holly smiled. "That's cute."

"You're cute." Randy reached over and tweaked her nose.

"Oh brother." Jaycee rolled his eyes. "Not again."

Holly looked up as Randy parked the car in his parents' driveway. "We're here," he said.

⁂

"Holly, you are an amazing young woman." Randy's mother smiled as she joined them in the living room.

"I know, right?" Randy grinned, leaning back on the couch. He wished Holly would have sat with him, but she'd opted for the rocking chair. Probably to keep distance between them. She was wise.

"We have been trying to get this kid to go see his Amish grandparents for quite some time. Nope. He'd never listen to any of us. All of a sudden, he discovers you, and he's willing to go to the moon."

"Mom." Randy shook his head. "Really?"

"You're rearranging your college schedule to be close to her too. That's saying something." She shifted toward Holly. "He was dying to *go away* to college."

Holly simply smiled at their exchange.

His mom popped up from the couch. "I think I'll put

on some water for cocoa, then I think I'll go check on those boys."

"Good idea," Randy said as his mother disappeared into another room.

"Randy, will you bring in some wood for the fire, please?" Mom hollered from the kitchen. "We're running low. We could use more kindling too."

"Sure, Mom." He glanced at Holly and winked. "Duty calls."

"I can help." She shot up from the rocker.

"You might want to grab your coat and gloves. I don't think the snow's still coming down, but it's cold out there."

"Okay. I'll chop the kindling."

His head whipped around in her direction. "Really?"

"Yeah. I love doing that. I can wield a hatchet with the best of 'em."

He chuckled. "I'm looking forward to watching you."

She eyed his fitted Henley and lifted a brow. "As I am you."

"You're flirting with me." His grin widened as he slid his jacket on.

"Maybe."

Randy set the ax down, then bent to check the log he'd just split to be sure it had cut through. He turned his head just in time to see Holly deposit a handful of snow down the back of his jacket. His breath momentarily stole away as the freezing particles trickled down his shirt. "You know, where I come from there are consequences for bad behavior."

He scooped up a handful of snow, but Holly was already on the run. She ducked behind a bush, so he crept around it. It was a good thing he knew the landscape better than she did. He moved in closer.

"You wouldn't." She challenged, eyeing his handful of snow.

He smirked. "Wouldn't I?"

He brought his hand up and she squealed as she shimmied from between the two bushes. He lunged after her but missed, then took off in a full-fledged sprint.

She yelped as he threw another snowball at her, then tackled her to the ground, pinning her beneath him.

"Now I've got you where I want you." He grinned. Their breaths, shallow and laboring, swirled upward through the wintry cold. He nearly drowned in the depth of her mesmerizing eyes.

Did he see longing there?

"Oh no." He swallowed. "I-I think I might kiss you."

Her smile faltered, but she didn't rebuff his comment. Was that an invitation? Permission?

His heartbeat quickened.

"Randy Travis Stoltz! What do you think you are doing? Don't make me have to call Holly's mother."

He groaned. Mom would have to ruin the moment. But it was likely a good thing. Because he had no idea how Holly would have responded if he'd given in to his desires. He was pretty sure she'd never kissed anyone, whereas he had not only kissed several girls, he'd gone further than he cared to admit. He wasn't proud of his past. Especially in light of his relationship with Holly. He'd never met anyone like her.

And then there was her father. He wouldn't be able to give him a straight answer when they met for their weekly accountability/discipleship meeting. Would he forbid Randy from ever seeing his daughter again? He was already breaking the no-touch rule, although they were both fully clothed and he wasn't touching her inappropriately. But somehow, he didn't think her father would view their current position as innocent.

This whole courtship thing was going to be *a lot* harder than he thought.

He snapped out of his reverie when he noticed Holly giggling.

"What?" He grinned and freed her from his hold. He

glanced up and was relieved that Mom had gone inside.

"Randy Travis?"

He shrugged. "Yeah. Mom always liked his music."

"Randy Travis." She giggled.

"What's *your* middle name?"

"I don't have one."

He frowned. "You don't have a middle name? Why not?"

"I don't know. None of us kids have one."

"How many siblings do you have?"

"Seven."

"Seven? Really? How did I not know this?"

"A few of them are already married and out of the house."

"So there are five of you at home?"

"No, only one of *me*." She teased. "I have two younger sisters and two brothers. One of them, Jason, is your age."

"Jason?"

"I think you've met him before. At least, he knows you."

"Hmm...I don't remember him."

"Uh, I think his girlfriend Ansley left him for you when they were dating in high school." Her brow rose.

His mouth formed an O. Yeah, he remembered Ansley well. How could he not? They'd dated for nearly a year. One of those past relationships he wished he could redo.

Or forget altogether. Or undo. He nodded slowly. "I think I know who he is. He didn't like me very much, did he?"

"I don't know how he feels about you now, but there was definitely a time when he viewed you as an adversary."

Randy grimaced. "I was…uh…kind of a jerk back then. There are a lot of things I've done that I wish I could undo."

"Well, I think we've all done stuff we aren't proud of. But God gives us another chance anyway. If God can look past our mistakes, hopefully we can look past each other's."

Wow, this woman was truly amazing. What had he done to deserve her?

"Can I get that in writing for when I make future mistakes?"

Her laugh seemed melodic somehow. "Maybe. But you'd have to sign it too."

"Deal." Their eyes met and held and, once again, an overwhelming urge to kiss her coursed through him. He forced himself to break the love spell, as he reached down and filled his arm with wood.

Holly picked up the bucket containing the kindling she'd deftly split.

All of a sudden, Randy knew what he would do. He would buy a large bag of chocolate kisses. Every time he was tempted to kiss her, he'd give her a different type of kiss instead. She could either eat them or save them up to redeem on their wedding night.

A shiver of delight raced through him at the thought.

SIXTEEN

Holly pulled up to the Stoltzes' small farm, delighting in the snow-covered landscape. A fresh powdering overnight had caused the tree branches to bend under the weight of a thick layer of snow. Their cabin-style home with its cozy front porch—its railing now covered in white and Christmas lights twinkling along the fascia—looked like it could've come straight from the page of a glossy calendar. A wisp of smoke danced from the chimney and disappeared into the chilly evening air. She quickly pulled out her phone to capture the picturesque scene before heading to the warmth that was sure to await her inside.

The door swung opened before she had a chance to complete her knock.

"Holly! Come in before you turn into a snowman." Shannon pulled her inside, her countenance bright. "Or should I say snow woman?"

A rush of warmth enveloped Holly, and her senses indulged in a sweetness that seemed to waft through the kitchen. "It smells wonderful in here."

"Jaycee insisted we have cookies ready and waiting for you. Well, he *said* for you but I really think he wanted a few for himself too. That boy loves his sweets. But if you allow him to eat too many, you'll never get him to go to sleep."

"I'll keep that in mind." She followed Shannon toward the living room where a fire roared in the stone hearth.

The moment Holly stepped into the room, a small hand slipped into hers. She glanced down to see three-year-old Melanie. She hadn't even heard her approach. The little girl pulled her toward the cheerful tinsel-clad Christmas tree in the corner and pointed to an ornament.

"Baby Jesus." Melanie's entire face beamed.

Shannon chuckled. "I'm convinced that will *always* be her favorite Christmas ornament. Wesley bought it for her when she was one."

Wesley walked into the room with baby Olivia in his arms. "And she insists it's the first one to go on the tree. When it's time to take it down, she cries."

Holly's heart clenched. "Aww…poor thing."

"I love Baby Jesus." Melanie smiled as she touched the ornament affectionately.

Holly crouched down beside the precious little girl. "That's a very nice ornament. I like it too."

"Happy Birthday, dear Jesus!" Melanie sang the words. "Happy Birthday to You!"

"That's right." Holly grinned at the girl. "Christmas is when we celebrate when Jesus was born."

Wesley looked at Shannon. "You ready to go, babe?"

"Yes. Is Olivia all set?" Shannon took the baby from his arms and kissed her chubby cheek.

"Fresh diaper. She had her bath. I think she's good." He reached over and tweaked the little one's cheek.

"Okay." She turned to Holly. "Dinner is in the oven. It should be ready in about ten minutes. Brighton can show you where everything is. Their bed time is at nine o'clock, but the little ones usually go down a little earlier. There are kids' movies you can put on for them in the entertainment center, and we have a decent-sized game closet with all sorts of fun. Umm…" Shannon bit her fingernail. "Oh, don't worry about doing the dishes after supper or anything. That's Brighton and Jaycee's job. I wrote our numbers on the fridge and Wesley's parents' number too, just in case you need it for whatever."

"I think you've covered just about everything, *Mom*." Wesley chuckled.

"I know. I just didn't want to forget anything." Shannon looked around. "Oh, yeah. Olivia likes the tree, so you'll need to keep an eye on her to make sure she doesn't bring it down on top of herself. Again." Shannon frowned. "Or try to eat the ornaments."

Holly nodded and attempted to suppress a smile. "I think we'll be fine."

Wesley tugged the side of Shannon's shirt. "We're going to miss our show if we don't hurry."

"We're going to a theater to see a play. I'm so excited." Shannon beamed. "Let me just tell all the kids goodbye."

Wesley frowned. "I thought you did that already."

"I know, but we're leaving now."

"Okay. Be quick. I'm going to warm up the truck."

"I'll be there in a minute."

Holly watched their conversation, wondering how she might be when she had a family of her own. And to think that Shannon was a couple of years younger than she was with a houseful already.

She finally waved them off a few moments later, smiling as she pointed through the window with Olivia in her arms. "Say bye bye."

"Bye. Bye." The little one waved. Then, as if she just realized her parents had left, her lip began to quiver.

Oh no.

A distraction was in order. "Let's go see if Melanie has her dolls out."

Holly began walking toward the living room just as the kitchen timer went off.

The boys came rushing into the living room.

"Dinner!" Jaycee hollered.

"Right." Holly spun around and headed back toward the kitchen. "Let's put you in your highchair," she told Olivia.

"Someone's knocking on the door!" Jaycee sprung up from the table where he'd plopped himself down five seconds ago.

"Wait, Jaycee. Don't answer it. Let me check who it is."

"It's Uncle Randy!" He jumped up and down as he stared through the window.

"Oh." Suddenly, Holly's cheeks warmed. "Okay. I'll get it."

She rushed to the door and pulled it open.

Randy's jaw dropped the moment he laid eyes on her. "Holly? What are you doing here?"

"I'm babysitting for Wesley and Shannon." She smiled.

Randy looked up toward the sky and raised his arms. "Praise the Lord, I don't have to change diapers!" A look of relief washed over him. He stepped into the house and engulfed Holly in a dizzying embrace before she could protest.

"Come and eat with us, Uncle Randy," Brighton invited, as he helped little Melanie into her booster seat.

"You can sit by me!" Jaycee pulled out the chair next to him.

Randy finally released Holly, setting her feet back on the ground. "You've been the answer to all kinds of my prayers lately." He looked at her sheepishly. "Uh-oh. I wasn't supposed to do that, was I?"

Holly giggled, shaking her head. "Should we see what Shannon made us for dinner?"

"You don't have to ask me twice." Randy chuckled. "You need help?"

"Uh, sure. Do you know where the potholders are?"

He slid a drawer open next to the oven. "Right here. I'll get it."

"Oh, my. That smells delicious." Holly could almost taste the fried chicken and macaroni and cheese before she even sat down.

Randy set the two dishes on the table, the swirl of heat rising into the air.

"Hot," Melanie said, pointing to one of the dishes. "Don't touch."

"That's right." Holly nodded.

Each of the children held out their hands to the person next to them.

"Will you pray, Uncle Randy?" Brighton asked.

Randy caught Holly's eye and smiled. "Sure."

They all bowed their heads.

"I can't tell you how relieved I was when I showed up here tonight and saw you." Randy grinned, aching to reach over and take Holly's hand. "I guess Wesley didn't trust me to change diapers after all."

"Haven't you changed a diaper before?"

"Just the other day when Wesley coached me." He made a disgusted face. "I almost gagged."

Holly laughed. "Well, you'll eventually have to get used to it if you ever get married. They say the average newborn baby goes through about ten diapers a day. I hope you won't expect your wife to change them all."

"Ten diapers a day?" His voice screeched.

"Sometimes more. That's the average."

"How can anyone afford all those diapers?"

"I don't know. But I'm glad we live in a day and age where diapers are disposable. I couldn't imagine washing out diapers by hand."

Randy shivered. "I don't even want my mind to go there. Why are we talking about diapers again?"

Holly laughed and shrugged. "You brought it up."

"Change of subject. How about a game?"

"A game. A game." Jaycee jumped up and down. "Can I pick it?"

Randy eyed Holly and cocked a brow. "What do you think?"

"Sounds good to me." She smiled.

"It could be dangerous," he warned.

"Let's play this one. It's my favorite!" Jaycee held up a box.

"Twister again?" Brighton shook his head. "You always pick that one."

"Well, you can pick one too. Uncle Randy will let us play two games tonight," Jaycee asserted.

Randy laughed. "Oh? Uncle Randy will, huh?"

Jaycee's head bobbed up and down several times.

"That's fine, but Holly gets to pick the movie tonight."

Jaycee rolled his eyes. "It'll be a kissing one. I know it will."

"Unless you want to go to bed early." Randy teased.

"Did I ever tell you kissing movies are my favorite?" Jaycee's face brightened.

Randy chuckled. "Yeah, and my name is Santa Claus. Nice try, kid."

After an exciting round of Twister, in which Randy was sure he must have broken the "no touching" rule at least a dozen times, followed by an equally exciting game of Pictionary, they plopped down on the couch in preparation for the movie. Randy was so tempted to slip his arm over the back of the couch and around Holly's shoulders. But he would refrain.

"You guys aren't going to be kissing, are you? Because that's what my sister and Wesley does *all* the time." Jaycee's nose wrinkled. "It's so gross."

"Nope. No kissing going on here." Randy held his hands up.

"I ain't never gonna have a girlfriend," Jaycee proclaimed.

"Oh, I think you might change your mind once you get older."

"Nope." He shook his head. "Never."

Holly giggled. "Well, then I'm sure there will be a long list of girls that will be heartbroken."

"I want popcorn!" Jaycee declared.

"That sounds good." Randy looked at Holly, who nodded in agreement.

"Brighton and me know how to make it. C'mon, Bright." Jaycee shot up from his chair and raced to the kitchen.

Randy sat up. "I think I'll put more wood on the fire."

"Good idea." Holly smiled. "I'll go peek in on the

girls to make sure they're still asleep after all the racket we made."

While Holly was absent, Randy hurried to the kitchen to grab the bag he'd brought. It was very clear he was going to need it.

Fortunately, the movie had been enough distraction to keep Randy's mind occupied. But now that the children had all gone to bed and just the two of them sat drinking steaming wassail, he was tempted to move in closer. If they kissed at this point, who would even know besides the two of them? He'd better keep that thought to himself.

Instead, he reached into the bag he'd brought and grabbed a fist full of chocolate kisses. "Hold out your hands." He grinned.

She eyed him curiously, her smile growing, then did as told.

"Close your eyes."

"You're pretty demanding. But okay, I'll play along."

He turned her hands around so that her palms faced upward, then gently ran his fingers over them with his free hand, and he noticed she took a small intake of breath at his touch. He leaned close and whispered in her ear, and a smile played on her lips. "I want to give you something." He then deposited the chocolates into her hands.

"May I open my eyes now?"

"Yes." Randy grinned.

She giggled when she looked down at her hands. "Kisses?"

"Well, since I'm not allowed to give you the real thing…" He shrugged.

"Ah, you are so sweet." She looked at him sheepishly. "I want to kiss you too."

His eyes widened. "You do?"

"Very much so. Actually, I've wanted to ever since you made a fool out of yourself in Walmart."

His grin stretched and he chuckled. "I did, didn't I?"

"But it was endearing."

"I'd happily be a fool for you."

"You're so cute."

His lips twisted. "I picture *cute* as something small and helpless, like a baby."

"We always called the guys cute that we thought were handsome." She laughed. "It was meant as a compliment."

"So why didn't you just say handsome?"

"Because handsome wouldn't accurately describe you. Yes, you are handsome, but you're also fun and quirky and excitable. The word handsome just doesn't sum all those things up."

"But cute does?"

She nodded.

"I think you're cute." He winked, gliding the back his hand over her upper arm. "And I think I want to kiss you even more now."

She glanced down at his hand and swallowed. Her gaze flickered to his lips, and he knew she desired the same thing. But he wouldn't take a kiss without her permission. Instead, he brought her hand to his lips and kissed it. That was forbidden too, of course, but it wasn't a kiss on the mouth.

"Randy, I…" Her chest rose and fell, then she lifted a hand to his cheek.

A crackle in the fireplace distracted him momentarily, then he covered her hand with his own. "May I?"

She nodded ever so slightly, and that was all the permission he needed. He leaned toward her, his hand slipping behind her head. The moment his lips met hers, he knew he was in trouble. Her kiss was slow and tender and sweet, but he desired more when they broke apart.

"Holly…" his voice was hoarse. He coaxed her onto his lap and dared to claim her mouth again, delighting in the fact that she'd planted one of her hands on his chest, and allowed him to deepen the kiss. He took his sweet time kissing her thoroughly, not wanting the blissfulness to come to an end.

A jostling of the door drew their attention and Holly jumped to her feet. "I shouldn't…we shouldn't have."

He stood from the couch as well. "Holly, it's okay. We'll keep it between us, alright?" He kept his voice low.

She nodded.

They walked toward the kitchen and greeted Shannon and Wesley. He shook his head at his brother. "Did you plan this?" He pointed back and forth to himself and Holly.

"I think Shannon was a little worried about you watching the kids alone, so she asked Holly." Wesley smiled. "I think she thought I would cancel you but I figured *many hands make light work*."

"Say what?"

"It's an Amish saying, something *Mammi* Judy says every so often," Shannon explained.

"I like it," Holly chimed in.

"How did everything go?" Shannon asked Holly.

She tugged in her bottom lip and glanced at Randy. "Good."

"No problems?" Wesley's brow arched.

Randy shook his head, his gaze flickering to Holly. "None at all."

Wesley's eyes moved back and forth from Randy to

Holly, then back to Randy again. "Is there something you're not telling us?"

Randy hoped he was the only one who noticed the pink tinge on Holly's cheeks. "Nothing to tell. I think I'll walk Holly out."

"Good idea." Wesley looked at his wife. "I don't know about you, but I'm beat."

"We won't keep you from your bed then," Randy said. "You ready to go, Holly?"

"Yeah, I'm ready." She smiled, as she pulled her beanie over her tresses.

Shannon leaned in and gave Holly a hug. "Thank you so much. We forgot to grab cash from the ATM. Do you mind if we pay you at church on Sunday?"

"Oh, I wasn't expecting to get paid. The kids were good, and it was fun," Holly said.

"Still. Wesley insists."

"A workman is worthy of his hire," Wesley added.

"Hey, what about me?" Randy feigned offense as he slid his arms into his coat.

"I have a feeling Holly did all the work." Wesley smirked. "How many diapers did you change?"

"Okay, okay, point taken." He put his gloves on and looked to Holly, who was doing the same. "You ready to brave the cold?"

She nodded.

They said their final goodbyes, waving to Shannon and Wesley as they stepped out onto the porch. "I should have turned on our vehicles ten minutes ago, then they'd be nice and toasty."

She shook her head. "Nah. Mine takes forever to warm up. I'll be almost home when the heater is finally useful."

He opened her car door, but refrained from pulling her into his arms lest prying eyes were watching. "M'lady." He'd used his cowboy accent again.

"Why, thank you, fine sir." She bowed, then slid into her car.

"See you tomorrow night?"

"Lord willing, I'll be there."

He stared after her vehicle as it pulled out of his brother's driveway, then jumped into his own. Tomorrow evening couldn't arrive soon enough, but until then he'd be replaying their kisses over and over again in his head and likely be dreaming about them when his head hit the pillow tonight.

SEVENTEEN

Holly's brisk jog trickled to a slow walk as the treadmill came to an eventual stop. She blew out a breath, wiped her forehead with a hand towel, then stepped off the exercise machine. She stopped for a moment when the dizziness hit, then gulped down a quarter of the water in her bottle.

She would need a shower before she dressed and prepared for the evening's festivities. She couldn't wait to see Randy tonight. How she would refrain from kissing him again, she didn't know. It seemed like once they'd started down that path, deviating from it—or halting altogether—would be nearly impossible. Kissing Randy had felt even better than she had imagined—and she had a pretty good imagination. Dad would likely be disappointed, but he'd left the relationship decision making to her. After all, it was her life. And she was quite certain Randy would be her life mate.

She'd been pondering that since their kisses last night. Soon she'd need to share her secret with him. Well, it wasn't a true secret since her family knew, but nobody other than her parents and siblings and maybe one other person were privy to her personal matters.

Worry threatened to take hold of her. What if Randy changed his mind about their relationship once he knew the truth? If he were to, he'd have every right end things between them. She knew he deserved more than what she could give him, but there were some things in life that one didn't have much control over. You just had to live the best you could and leave the results up to God. *Which is why you shouldn't worry about it*, Mom had reminded her in the past.

But she *did* worry about it. Because she desired to be open and honest with Randy. Because she feared what his reaction might be. Because losing the man she'd fallen in love with would completely break her.

Randy's pulse quickened the moment he spotted Holly's vehicle entering the church parking lot. Since he'd never been to a church singles group event, he'd waited in his car until Holly arrived. Spending another evening with her would be a dream. If only they could steal away for a few moments and indulge in a kiss or two. Did Holly regret kissing him last night? Or did she, like him, relive those few precious moments over and over again in her mind?

He stepped out of his car the moment her vehicle rolled to a stop, then walked over and opened her door. The moment he did, his senses filled with everything Holly. Her gentle but intoxicating perfume. Her bright smile that rarely seemed to dim. Her fabulous wardrobe that complimented her complexion perfectly. "You look gorgeous."

"Hi to you too." She smiled, taking his hand as he assisted her exit from the vehicle. "I hope you brought a scarf. It might get cold tonight."

"Uh-oh." He grimaced.

They headed toward the entrance of the fellowship hall. "I'm sure it'll be fine. At least you brought a warm coat."

He glanced down at his wool trench coat. "That, I did. I'm not overdressed, am I?" Although his coat was a little fancy, he'd worn jeans and flannel underneath.

"It's perfect for caroling. And it looks great on you."

Her compliment warmed him from the inside out.

He held the door to the fellowship hall open for her, wishing they could find a secluded place to talk. They hadn't discussed the kiss at all last night, and he was dying to know Holly's thoughts on the matter. She didn't seem to be upset about it. Yet, at the same time, it wasn't supposed to happen.

What on earth would her father think? Would he change his mind about allowing Randy to court his daughter? Had Holly confessed their tender moments to her father or had she kept them to herself? He hoped the answer was the latter scenario.

But Holly had given him permission to kiss her. He hadn't—he wouldn't have—stolen a kiss from her, knowing how she felt. Which was why he'd asked, and why he was ever-so-thankful she'd wanted the same thing.

All of a sudden, he remembered his accountability meeting he had scheduled with her father next week. He smacked his forehead. How on earth could he not confess what he'd done?

"Are you okay?" Holly waved a hand in front of his face.

He blinked, then realized his surroundings. "Yeah, sorry." He leaned close to her ear. "I was thinking about my meeting with your father next week."

She nodded, seemingly unworried.

"I don't know what I'm going to tell him." He swallowed.

"He values honesty."

"I've never been all that great at keeping the rules."

"Nah, really?" She giggled. "I never would have guessed."

"Am I that easy to read?"

"Hmm…let me see. There was the ice skating rink with your then-girlfriend. The incident at Walmart. Your grandparents. Driving up and down the roller coaster road at crazy speeds. And then…last night," she whispered the last part.

"I guess you have a point."

"And we've known each other all of a week."

He chuckled. "I can't seem to help myself. Especially around you."

"Which is exactly why we're courting *with* chaperones."

"Yeah, because when it's just the two of us…"

She tugged in her bottom lip, and color rose in her cheeks. "Yeah."

"I guess I'm not the only rule breaker." He winked.

A clapping sound stole their attention. He looked at the man who'd clapped, recognizing him as a member of the church who sometimes ushered. "If you would all gather around now, I'd like to say a quick prayer before we start."

He and Holly moved toward the front of the room. Each person in their group held out their hand to the person next to them, then they all bowed their heads.

The man in charge led out, "Dear gracious Heavenly Father, we come before You today in adoration and praise and with thankful hearts. You, oh God, in Your love, have sent Your precious Son, Jesus, to this earth for us. Please be with us this evening as we endeavor to share that love with others in the community. Help us to be Your hands and feet. Help us to be that blessing that somebody needs tonight. Please give us safety tonight as we navigate the slick roads. We ask all this in the mighty wonderful name of Jesus. Amen."

All of sudden, Randy felt like shouting. It was almost like he could feel the Spirit of God in the room with them. It was simply amazing.

"Make sure to grab a snack or two from the kitchen, and a warm beverage, before we head out. We have a list on the table there. I'd like each of you to pick one home in the community that you'd like to stop at. Think of who might enjoy caroling the most. Or maybe just a friend or loved one who doesn't know the Lord," the leader said.

Randy turned to Holly. "Do you know whose house you'll pick?"

Her smile widened. "Yes."

"I was thinking Wesley's kids would get a kick out of seeing carolers. I don't know if they've ever seen them before in real life, only in the movies."

"Good idea. They'll love it."

"What about you?"

She shrugged. "Well, we used to go to my grandparents' house. But Grandpa Remington died a few years ago and we lost Grandma earlier this year, so…" She grew quiet when tears welled in her eyes.

"I'm sorry."

"No, it's okay. We all gotta die sometime, right?" She swiped at her tears. "I just miss them."

That was something Randy couldn't relate well to, he realized. He'd never had anyone close to him pass away. Not like his sister-in-law Shannon, who'd lost both of her parents in one fell swoop and instantly became sole caretaker of her three younger siblings. No, he'd been quite oblivious to that depth of grief. He'd been blessed, he now realized. What would it be like to experience that kind of pain, that kind of loss? He wasn't looking forward to finding out.

EIGHTEEN

Holly, Randy, and their entire singles group tromped through the snow and piled back into the church van. "Is everyone still having a good time?" their leader, Eddie, asked.

Everyone responded positively.

"Not too cold?"

"Nah, we're fine," one of their group members said.

Holly knew she was fine. Especially when she got to cuddle close to Randy in the van.

Eddie looked down at his clipboard. "Okay. We just have two more places to visit." He zeroed in on Randy. "We'll visit your people first, then we'll wrap up with Holly's."

Randy nodded, slipping his arm around her shoulder. Holly leaned in as close as she could to absorb as much of his warmth as possible.

Not ten minutes later, they pulled into Wesley and Shannon's driveway.

"This ought to be fun." Excitement danced in Randy's eyes.

"I think you might enjoy this more than Jaycee will," Holly teased.

"Oh, I know I will. I get to stand next to the most beautiful girl in the world." His gloved hand grazed her cheek.

She stared up at him, wishing they were the only two people in the van. "You're a flatterer, you know that?"

He lifted his hands in defense. "Hey, I only tell the truth, little lady." His southern drawl was back.

She smiled in spite of herself.

"You two coming?" One of the guys in the row behind them gestured for them to exit ahead of him.

"Yep." Randy stood, guiding Holly by the hand toward the other carolers awaiting them outside.

As they had done at the previous residences they'd visited, the group quietly walked up to the home's entrance, formed a semi-circle, then began with the first line of "Hark the Herald Angels Sing." Holly glanced at Randy, who winked when he caught her looking. His voice rang out just as loud as the others, even though he lacked confidence in his singing ability. But Holly thought he sounded just fine. As far as she could tell, he hadn't sung off-key or anything. And if he had, it wouldn't have bothered her. The Bible said to make a joyful noise. God looked on the heart.

Halfway into the first line of the song, Wesley opened the door. Soon, Shannon and most of the children joined him. Holly guessed the youngest was likely in bed already. Jaycee and Brighton sung along as they moved on to "Jingle Bells," then "Silent Night." They ended the ensemble with "We Wish You a Merry Christmas."

A designated caroler handed out candy canes, along with a copy of the Biblical Christmas story.

Soon, they said their goodbyes and piled back into the van, heading to their final destination.

"Did you tell me whose house you picked?" Randy stared at her.

She shook her head and lifted a mischievous grin. "You'll see."

"Wait. We're not…" He leaned forward in the seat and tried to make out which road they were on. It was a little hard to tell since everything had been covered in white. "I know where we are. We're going to my grandparents' house, aren't we?"

She shrugged.

"I know we are." His brow furrowed. "You do realize that they turn in for bed around seven, right?"

"You're kidding."

"Nope. We'll probably wake them up."

Holly bit her fingernail. "Do you think they'll mind?"

"Beats me. I guess we'll find out in a few more minutes."

Christopher awoke to a rocking motion. His *fraa's* hand shook his shoulder until he fully awakened. "Christopher, what's that sound I hear?"

"It sounds like the angels in my dream."

"It's singing, ain't not? Go see who's here."

He rolled out of bed, then lit the lantern on the nightstand. He yanked his shirt on, then pulled on his suspendered pants his *fraa* had lovingly sewn for him some years ago. He wouldn't bother with shoes.

He ambled toward the front door, lantern in hand. He pulled the door open. To his delight, his *gross sohn* Randy and his *aldi* stood outside singing with several other *youngie.*

"Who is it, Christopher?" Judy called from behind him.

"It's Randy and his *aldi*, with some others," he quietly called over his shoulder.

"Well, invite them in. They must be freezing out in that air."

"They're singing, *fraa.*"

"Well, they can sing inside. Have them come in and I'll ready some water for coffee."

"As you wish, *fraa*." He chuckled. "Why don't you put some popcorn on, too?"

"*Gut* idea."

Christopher beckoned the group inside, holding the door open until each one entered. "Have a seat." He gestured toward the benches. Then he moved to pull a few extra chairs in from the living room.

The group continued to sing Christmas songs, then their joyous melodies finally came to a halt.

"Thank you. We enjoyed that very much," Judy said as she set a large bowl of popcorn on the table. "Help yourselves. I'm making a second batch right now."

"And there's hot water for anyone who'd like coffee," Christopher offered.

"I'll take some," his *gross sohn* said.

Judy set several mugs and spoons on the table, along with a pot of hot water with a ladle, a jar of instant coffee, a Mason jar of cold milk, and a bowl of white sugar.

Several of his *kinskind's* friends indulged in food and beverage as well. Each one seemed very appreciative and polite.

"Well, what a way to end the evening. This is a blessing," the oldest one from the group said. "We appreciate your hospitality, sir, ma'am."

Almost a half hour later, the group said their farewells and thanked them again for the snacks. Judy managed to send each one off with a small bag of her cookies.

After Christopher closed the door, he turned to his *fraa*. "Well, that was a pleasant surprise, *ain't so?*"

"*Jah*. It is always a blessing to see our *gross sohn*. It seems like he might be finally coming around."

"It was his *aldi's* idea to come here, he said."

"She is a good one, that young lady."

"Holly is what he said her name was."

"I'll have to try and remember that."

Christopher nodded. "I have a feeling she might be the one *Der Herr* has picked out for our *gross sohn*."

"She seems to be perfect for him." Judy yawned. "I don't know about you, husband, but I plan to count a few more sheep before the sun rises."

"I'm right behind you, *fraa*."

"Your grandparents are amazing," Holly spoke the words into Randy's warm coat, which currently enveloped both of them.

The others in their singles group had emptied out the parking lot five minutes ago, leaving only the two of them. Holly didn't want to say goodbye.

Randy stroked her hair. "You think so?"

"I love them. They remind me of my grandparents." She stared up into his eyes. "I'm so glad you reconnected with them."

The corner of his mouth lifted and his fingers slid over her cheek. He leaned down and claimed a kiss, his breath a mixture of coffee and peppermint. "What would your father say if he saw us like this?"

She shrugged. "He'd probably warn us to be careful."

"You don't think I'd be reprimanded for kissing you?"

"Maybe. I'm sure he'd say we're rushing into things."

"I think I might be addicted to you. When we're not together, I want to be with you. You're all I think about." He shook his head. "I've never felt this way about anybody."

"I feel the same way."

He sighed. "I wish I had my act together so I could marry you."

Her eyes widened and she stepped back, but not out of his embrace. "Really? Randy, I think it's too soon. We don't even know each other well."

"I feel like you know me. I mean, what's there to know?"

"I have no idea what your favorite color is—"

"Blue."

"Or your favorite food—"

"You *do* know that one. Spaghetti." He grinned.

"Good. Because spaghetti's easy to make." She smiled, and he leaned down to kiss the tip of her nose.

"What's yours?"

"My favorite color is purple. My favorite food is…" Her lips twisted. "I don't know if I have a favorite food, actually. I like most things. Mexican, Italian, Chinese, American, seafood."

"Me too. I'm not picky. So you could probably make me tofu surprise and I'd eat it."

She smiled. "Really? Because I have a lot of great tofu recipes."

"I was kind of joking. But I'm definitely willing to try them. Especially if you're the one making the meal."

"You're so easy. I love that about you. You seem to just go with whatever comes your way."

"Aah, for the most part, I guess. What about you?"

"Not so much. I have strong opinions about things, especially where morality is concerned."

He nodded. "Hence, wanting me to reconcile with my Amish grandparents."

"Right. And I tend to be skeptical about things."

"Like what?"

She shrugged. "Whatever, really. I mean, if I hear something, I'll want to look it up and research to make sure what I'm hearing is accurate. I don't take a lot of things at face value, because there are usually underlying facts that you never hear."

"Did you research me?" He raised his eyebrows twice.

"No. I think you're pretty transparent."

"Really?"

"Yes."

"What about you?" His fingers wiggled against her, tickling her side. "Do you have secrets?"

She giggled at the motion. "Maybe."

"Maybe?" He stepped back, examining her. "Uh-oh. I don't know if I like you keeping secrets from me."

"I'll divulge them when the time is right." She winked.

"A woman of mystery." He eyed her cautiously. "I mean, it's not like something major, right? Like, you're not already married or anything?"

She laughed and playfully slapped his arm. "Randy Travis Stoltz, what kind of girl do you think I am?"

"So you *are* married," he teased, pulling her close for a kiss. "Your husband isn't going to like me very much then."

"Stop that. What if someone overhears? They might get the wrong idea."

"The wrong idea? That you're cheating on your husband?"

"You." She shook her head. "What am I going to do with you?"

He leaned down and claimed another kiss. "Oh, I don't know. Divorce your husband and marry me?"

She giggled. "I think I might do that. Someday."

NINETEEN

*C*hurch had been amazing.

Church had been amazing? If Randy didn't know better, he'd think he had become a different person. Because, it wasn't just the fact that Holly had been standing beside him. He honestly loved every part of the service. From the singing, to the testimonies, to the fellowship, to the preaching, it felt like God had been present and moving. Truthfully, he didn't think he'd *ever* experienced being in God's house like this. Was this what he'd been missing out on?

It seemed it took a wonderful woman like Holly to open his eyes to everything that God had for him. Namely, a real relationship with his Creator. When he'd gone home and opened his Bible, after his awesome night with Holly and the singles group, it seemed like the words had jumped off the page and into his heart. He now reminisced on the passage from Ephesians chapter three. About how God talked about the riches of His glory, and about knowing His strength and His power that dwelled inside the hearts of believers. Randy was certain that's what was happening.

Life was exciting. His college party days paled in comparison to the life he was now living. Those days had always left him feeling empty. But now, he had a feeling of completeness, a feeling of confidence and overwhelming joy. As the song they'd sang earlier, "Joy Unspeakable and Full of Glory." He wished it would never fade away.

Holly's voice yanked him from his musings. "My dad's grilling out. Do you like steak and chicken?"

"No tofu?" He snapped his fingers and frowned. "I guess steak and chicken will have to do." He sighed heavily.

Holly giggled. He loved the sound of her voice. She almost always seemed happy. Except when she'd been put out with him.

"You know you've found the right girl when she laughs at your jokes." He squeezed her hand.

"You ready to go?"

He patted his stomach. "My tummy is already rumbling."

"Your tummy? I think helping me teach Sunday school and being around the children is rubbing off on you." She giggled. "I know. I heard it during church. Didn't you eat breakfast?"

"At my mom's insistence, yes. But, truthfully, I was a little nervous about today, so I didn't eat all that much."

"You? Nervous?"

"I know you thought I was super human, but alas, my armor's cracks have emerged."

She shook her head. "Are you always this entertaining?"

"Afraid not. Eight hours a day I'm out like a light."

"Well, no doubt, during those sleeping hours your mind is conjuring up clever things to say." She gestured toward her parents. "I'm going to see if they mind if I ride with you."

He rubbed his hands together. "Now we're talking."

An hour later, Holly and her mom cleared the lunch dishes from the table.

"What can I do to help?" Randy offered. "My mom says I'm an expert dish washer."

"Why don't you come join me in the den?" her father said. "I've got a nice fire going in there. We can chat."

Holly caught the worried look in Randy's eye. She lifted a reassuring smile.

He followed her father into the den, but Holly tried to keep a pulse on the conversation, just in case she needed to rescue Randy.

"How are things going with you and Holly?" she heard her father ask.

"Amazing," was Randy's enthusiastic response.

"My daughter tells me the two of you have decided to discard the courtship rules?"

Holly imagined Randy cringing about now.

"Well, actually, not totally. We're still doing the chaperoned dates."

"But not completely chaperoned," her father stated.

"Uh, no. But we've agreed on some rules."

"Like?"

"Like saving…uh…intimacy for marriage. And not touching inappropriately," he added.

"Where do you see yourself a year from now? I know I asked that before, but have your plans changed?"

"Hopefully, married to your daughter, sir."

"Just Bruce is fine."

"Okay, Bruce." Randy continued, "I've kind of rearranged my plans. In addition to finishing my degree, I'd like to get a part-time job so I can save up for a down payment on a house."

Holly's heart flipped at his words. Being married to Randy would be like a fairy tale.

"Marriage isn't like a fairy tale." Had her father just read her mind? "I know it seems that way now, but you and Holly will encounter many difficult things. There will be times when you will disagree and argue. There will be times when your will, or Holly's, or both, will have to bend. You'll face hardships. It could be the death of a child. It could be a complete financial disaster caused by a tornado or a storm that leaves you homeless. Will your commitment survive when everything is seemingly against you? Are you willing to hold on when it seems like there's nothing to hold on to?"

"I would hope that our faith in God would get us through those situations, should they come our way."

"Now would be a good time to get into the Word. Strengthen your faith and memorize some Scripture verses that will help you weather those storms. Like John 14:27."

"What does it say?"

"*Peace I leave with you, my peace I give unto you: not as the world giveth, give I unto you. Let not your heart be troubled, neither let it be afraid.*"

"Wow. That's a great verse."

"Also, John 16:33. *These things I have spoken unto*

you, that in me ye might have peace. In the world ye shall have tribulation: but be of good cheer; I have overcome the world."

"Those are both encouraging verses. Thank you for sharing them."

"The fact is, a lot of people get saved and think that their troubles will disappear. But the opposite is often true, because those living for Jesus basically have a large bullseye on their back. Satan's going to try his best to knock us off our feet. He knows that if we are down or distracted, we won't be doing anything for the kingdom of God. But we are not ignorant of his devices."

"What are his devices?"

"It could be any number of things. Distraction. Fear. Discouragement. Anger. Lust. Envy. Any type of sin we allow into our lives. We need to keep our eyes fixed on Jesus. I'm confident that the end, and His coming, are nearer than we think."

"Wow. That's a lot to consider."

"Someone once summed it up this way: *Only one life, it soon will pass. Only what's done for Christ will last.* When we get to the end, that will be all that matters, according to 1 Corinthians chapter three. After salvation, of course."

"That sounds pretty intense."

"Not that there won't be great and wonderful times. There are plenty of those too. The Bible also says to rejoice with the wife of thy youth. I'll let you read the rest of that passage on your own."

Holly peeked around the corner in time to see her father wink at Randy.

"What do you mean by that?" Randy grinned.

"Look up Proverbs chapter five when you get home."

"Proverbs five. Okay, I'll try to remember."

"Oh, you won't forget it once you've read it." Her father chuckled. "But be sure to read 1 Corinthians 7:1 for good measure. That verse applies to you *now*."

Holly recalled what the passage from Proverbs said, and her cheeks immediately warmed at the thought of Randy reading it in the context of their relationship.

She bit her fingernail, contemplating whether or not she should interrupt. A hand on her shoulder told her that Mom was standing behind her.

Mom leaned close and whispered, "Are you eavesdropping again?"

She turned around and faced her mother, stepping further into the kitchen. "Mom, Dad just mentioned Proverbs five," she whispered.

Mom smiled. "Well, it *is* part of the Bible."

"I know, Mom. But really?"

Mom captured her attention by resting her hand on Holly's forearm. "Are you planning on telling him soon?"

Holly looked away. "I don't know."

"Sooner is better than later. Randy seems like he might be in it for the long haul."

"I know. I just…he doesn't take disappointment well."

"Then I suggest you pray about it. But you should tell him." Mom held her gaze. "Soon."

TWENTY

"Would you like a tour of our home?" Holly offered.

"Sure." Randy smiled. "Hey, where are all your siblings? How come I never see them in church?"

"Oh. Well, we've only been going to that church for about four years. They still attend our former church. Our aunt and cousins go there as well, and they invited them over today." Holly led the way up a carpeted staircase.

"So, you have aunts and uncles in the area?"

"Yes. You?" They stopped at the top of the stairs.

"No. My grandparents and aunts and uncles all live in either Arkansas or Oklahoma. With the exception of my Amish grandparents, of course."

"So, for Christmas and Thanksgiving it's just you guys?"

"It had been up until a couple of years ago when my Amish grandparents started joining us. I pretty much always kept my distance from them, though." He looked down a hallway. "How many bedrooms are up here?"

"Six. We all have our own rooms now. My parents' bedroom is downstairs." She moved to a door. "This is my brother Jason's bedroom. I can't guarantee that any of these are going to be clean." She grimaced.

"It doesn't bother me. I've made some pretty big messes in the past."

"Why do I believe you?" She giggled.

She opened the door, which revealed a decently organized room. After that, she walked across the hall to her other brother's room. Then she continued, until she came to the last one. "I chose this as mine because I thought it would be the quietest."

"Is it?" He peered into her abode. The feminine pillows and curtains indicated it was certainly a girl's bedroom.

She stepped inside and Randy followed. "As quiet as can be with seven people living in one house."

"Have you told them about us?" He felt his brow quirk.

"Yeah, they know." She gestured toward her desk chair. "You may have a seat. We just need to keep the door open. Mom and Dad's rules."

He studied her bed. "Is your bed slanted?"

"Oh. Uh, yeah. It's a wedge. That's how I sleep."

"Really? Why?"

"I…I guess maybe now might be a good time to tell you." Her gaze drifted to the floor.

"Tell me what?"

"The secret I mentioned?"

"Ah, the husband."

She smiled, shook her head, then walked to her desk and opened the top drawer. She pulled out what looked to be a few papers that had been stapled together, and held them in her hands. "I have something called cardiomegaly."

He blinked and shook his head. "What is that?"

"It's also known as an enlarged heart. Basically, my heart muscles don't work properly." She handed him the information, then sat on the corner of her bed. "Sleeping flat could…create problems."

Randy attempted to process her words. He stared down at the papers she'd given him, but they seemed to blur. "What does that mean? I mean…is it…it sounds serious." He stared at her. He needed answers.

"It's all in the papers." When she gestured to them, he realized her hands were shaking. Why were her hands shaking?

He forced himself to focus on the papers and began reading silently, *An enlarged heart is not a disease, but might be a sign of heart disease. An enlarged heart cannot pump blood properly and could cause complications that lead to sudden stroke or congestive heart failure.* He skimmed the next few lines. *Life expectancy depends on cause. Doctors don't always know the cause. Even with treatment, patient has a downhill battle. Severe heart disease patients can die within a few years.*

Randy stopped reading, dropping the papers onto her desk as though they'd scalded him. If only that were the case. If only that were the worst of his predicament. His chest clenched tightly, like *he* was the one with heart failure.

The ticktock of the purple clock on her nightstand seemed to grow louder with each second that passed. Tick. Tock. Tick. Tock.

He stared at Holly until he could no longer see her. "So…" his voice trembled and he hated it. "What you're saying is…what you're saying is…there's a very good chance you could *die* soon?" He shoved away his tears.

"I don't know, Randy." Moisture gathered in her eyes as well. "Yes. I guess it's possible."

"But I thought we were…" He frowned. "What are we even doing here?"

"What do you mean?"

He shot up from the chair. "What's the point of our

relationship if it's going to just end like that?" He hadn't meant to raise his voice, but under the circumstances...

Tears trickled down her cheeks. "What are you saying, Randy?"

"How could you let me go on and on about getting married, about believing we had a future and..." He shook his head, doing his best to repress his grief but failing miserably. Disappointment, disillusionment, and despair strangled him all at once, and he was desperate to escape.

Randy moved to the bedroom door.

Holly stood from the bed. "Are you leaving?"

"I don't know. Yes. I guess I just need time to process all this." He rushed from her bedroom. He hurried down the stairs. He sprinted out the door to his car. He turned over the ignition and sped out of her driveway. And he did all of it without a second thought. Because if he stopped to think, he'd have to face reality.

His precious Holly...was dying.

TWENTY-ONE

Two hours later, Randy found himself pulling into his grandparents' driveway. He'd spent the last hour pouring his aching heart out to Mom and Dad. He was certain he'd cried more in the last two hours than he had in his entire life—including when he was a baby. Mom had even agreed on that point.

Randy didn't know why his father had suggested he come here, but Dad had said to trust him. And so he did.

He cut the engine, then walked up to the house. This was the first time he'd ever been here at the farm alone.

His grandmother opened the door at his knock. "*Kumm* in." She looked beyond him, but must've realized he was flying solo today. Like he very well might be for the rest of his life. The thought caused his heart to squeeze tightly. Tears threatened, although he doubted he had many more to spare.

His grandfather beckoned Randy to join him in the living room. It must've been ninety degrees in the house. He glanced to where the large black and silver stove sat, several feet from him, and realized he better divest himself of his outer clothing lest he experience a heat stroke.

"You come all alone today?" His grandfather set his newspaper to the side and focused on Randy.

"Yeah."

"Where's your *aldi*, your girlfriend?"

He inhaled deeply, then expelled the air. "Holly and I are sorta taking a break right now, I guess you can say."

"I see."

He squeezed his eyes closed. "She dropped a bombshell on me, and I'm having a difficult time processing it. Dad suggested I come talk to you. I'm not even sure why."

"I see. A bombshell, you say?" His brow furrowed, and Randy realized he needed to explain.

His grandmother brought him cookies and a cup of steaming coffee. How could anyone drink hot coffee in this inferno? He thanked his grandmother, nonetheless.

"She's…" he swallowed hard. It was difficult to even say the words. "Holly has a heart condition. She…uh…she could die suddenly…at any time. I just don't know how I'm going to deal with that when it actually happens."

"I see." His grandfather nodded. "We must place our lives and the lives of our loved ones in *Der Herr's* hands."

"*Der Herr?*"

"The Lord," his grandpa clarified. "*He* is the one who determines when it is we will leave this earth. None of us know when that day will be. *You* could even die before your *aldi*. Today even."

"You're right, of course. But the chances of Holly dying sooner are much greater than mine."

His grandfather reached for a Bible that sat with several other books on a small table. "Listen to what *Gott* says here." He opened the Bible, then handed the large tome to Randy. "Read the first part." He pointed to a verse.

Randy looked down at the words. "Be still, and know that I am God."

"That's it. That is the sum of what we must do, as His *kinner*, his children. We must be still. We must trust that He is *Gott* and we are not." His grandfather pointed upward. "He knows best."

"That's hard to do."

"When your *grossmudder* and I lost Katie and Kendal, we were devastated. They were your aunt and uncle." Randy noted the tenderness in his grandfather's voice as he continued. "Your *vatter* was the only one of our *kinner* to survive the accident. And then when he chose to leave the *g'may*, our church family, it was as if we had lost all three of our *kinner*."

Randy frowned. "Why didn't you have more? I thought Amish people had large families."

"*Nee*. Your *grossmudder* was injured in the accident, and we couldn't have any more." He sat stalwart, as though the stance absorbed his pain somehow. "We'd hoped for at least a dozen. But when it was all said and done, we were left with none."

He couldn't imagine. He took a bite of the delicious chocolate chip cookie.

"*Sohn*, don't worry about what *might* happen in the future. You have today. You have now. Enjoy each day *Der Herr* gives you with your *aldi*. And if *Gott* is willing, perhaps she will one day become your *fraa*."

He arched a brow. "*Fraa*?"

His grandfather chuckled. "Wife."

Randy closed his eyes and inhaled deeply. "That would be a dream. But Holly might not even have that long."

"Have you read the story of Hezekiah in the Bible?"

"Hezekiah?" His brow lowered. "No, I don't think so. Is it in the book of Hezekiah?"

His grandfather chuckled for some reason.

"What?" Randy almost smiled.

"There is no book of Hezekiah in the Bible."

"Oh. There isn't?"

"No. But you can find his story in 2 Chronicles. I mention him because he prayed to God to let him live longer, and God granted him fifteen more years. Have you prayed for your *aldi*?"

"Yes, I have." *That* he could say with confidence.

"When you pray, you must have faith that *Gott* will answer."

Randy nodded. "I try to."

"Is there no cure for this heart condition? No treatment?"

"I don't know, actually. I didn't read all the papers Holly gave me. I was so upset, I just left."

Holly had attempted to call him several times, but he couldn't bring himself to answer his phone.

"She looked healthy when she was here. Vibrant, even," his grandfather remarked.

"I know. She has a very good disposition for someone who's dying." He thought on his grandfather's words. "You know, I think I'll do some research on the internet when I get home."

"Can you stay for supper?" his grandmother chimed in. "It's just about ready."

"That would be great, Grandma. Thank you." Randy smiled for the first time since learning of Holly's condition.

His grandmother affectionately returned his smile when he said "Grandma" in reference to her—for the first time ever.

They each took their seats at the table, then bowed their heads. Randy had learned about the silent prayer from Wesley, so he'd known what to expect.

He enjoyed a meal of buttered noodles, homemade bread with fresh butter and jam, and sliced meat. It wasn't fancy by any means, but it was delicious nonetheless and hit the spot.

When he left an hour later, it seemed like a bit of the heaviness had lifted from his shoulders. He'd embraced both of his grandparents and thanked them. And he graciously accepted an invitation for him and Holly to join them for what they'd called Second Christmas.

TWENTY-TWO

Holly had been in a melancholy mood since Randy stormed out of the house yesterday. She knew he would need time to process the news, but she never dreamed he'd fall apart. She'd been praying nonstop since he left. In truth, she worried about him. If she'd read the expression on his face and interpreted his brusque actions correctly, he'd been completely devastated by her revelation.

She wondered how he was coping. How long would it be before he came around again? *Would* he come around again? Just thinking of the possibility that he might not return grieved her. What if he decided it was too much to deal with? What if he avoided her altogether and went away to college like he'd originally planned? What if he never came back?

He hadn't even answered her calls. That alone had been a pretty good indication of his intentions.

She sighed heavily, but forbade the tears that threatened. Never had she cared so deeply for a man.

"Holly? Honey, are you planning to eat breakfast?" Mom called from the stairs.

Both her mother and father had been worried about her after Randy had left so abruptly. She'd assured them that she'd be okay, but she wasn't being truthful. The truth was that her heart ached like it never had before. And she wasn't sure that sort of thing didn't have an effect on her condition. She wasn't supposed to get worked up, but the situation made that scenario impossible for Holly.

"I'm coming, Mom," she called back.

She knew one thing. If Randy didn't return, this would be the most miserable Christmas ever.

An hour after Holly had finished breakfast, she heard a noise outside the door. "Mom, I think someone might be here." She dried the last few dishes and stuck them in the cupboard.

"It's for you, Holly." Mom glanced at Holly briefly and lifted a reassuring smile, then left the room.

She frowned when she heard jostling in the

doorway. Her eyes widened when Randy bumbled through the door, several grocery bags hanging from each arm. "Randy? What is this?"

"I was up all night researching your condition. Holly, it's not only treatable, but it's curable!" He set the bags on the table, then pulled her into his arms. "I'm sorry for leaving the way I did yesterday. Forgive me?"

She nodded, her chin suddenly wobbly. He hadn't left her.

"None of that. We're done crying, okay?" He glanced behind her, probably to make sure Mom wasn't there, then cradled her face in his hands and kissed her on the mouth. He leaned back and stared into her eyes intently. "I love you. So much."

Her heart melted at his words. She wished he'd hold her in his arms forever.

But he released her, focused on the task at hand, and began emptying the grocery bags.

"What is all this, Randy?"

"This is your prescription for wellness. I also ordered some stuff online." He pulled out the contents one by one. "Grapes are wonderful for heart health. I tasted them at the store to make sure they weren't sour. I don't think the worker at Kroger appreciated it very much, but oh well. I wasn't going to bring you sour grapes."

She giggled. *Always breaking the rules*.

He continued, holding up two bottles. "Grape juice. Orange juice. Vitamin C is excellent for a healthy heart." He held up a couple of tea boxes. "This is Echinacea tea. It's a great immune system booster, I learned. As is Elderberry. I also bought you some heart syrup that you can take on a daily basis."

"Randy, this is too much."

"Nope. You are not *even* going to argue with me. I refuse to let you die. Not on *my* watch. So help me God, I'm going to do everything in my power to keep you alive and healthy." He held up a finger. "Oh, and I'll need those chocolate kisses back. They're not good for you. The real thing is much better anyhow." He winked mischievously.

Tears surfaced in her eyes. No man had ever loved her like this.

"I want to take care of you, Holly. I'll do whatever it takes." He pulled out some papers. "Here, I want you to read this. It's a story about a young guy who was born with a heart condition. He was in the hospital and going to have surgery, but after another young man died on the operating table, he ran out of the hospital. I won't tell you the whole story, but he ended up curing his heart condition—something the doctors had told him was incurable."

"Dr. Schulze?"

His jaw slacked. "You know about him?"

She smiled. "Yes."

His enthusiasm deflated. "So, you already knew all this?"

Her smile widened. "Yes. I pretty much eat a mostly vegetarian diet." She reached into the cupboard, and handed Randy a container.

He read the label. "Dr. Schulze's Superfood."

She nodded. "I try to take it every day."

"And exercise? I read that it's important to keep your heart pumping the way it should, but not to overdo it."

"I walk on the treadmill every day."

He shook his head, then pulled her close again. "So, what you're telling me is, I was worried for nothing?"

"No, not for nothing." Her smile evaporated. "I still do have cardiomegaly. But I'm doing what I can to fight it."

"That's my girl." He leaned down and claimed the kiss Holly had been aching to give him since he'd arrived.

TWENTY-THREE

"Ican hardly believe Christmas is already here." Holly snuggled in the comfort of Randy's arms, surrounded by his family. Earlier, they'd shared a meal and read about the birth of Jesus from the Bible. Later, they'd drive to her parents' place and enjoy Christmas dinner with them. Randy had unnecessarily kept an eagle eye on her, making sure she didn't indulge in anything that would compromise her health. She thought it was sweet the way he'd fussed over her.

"New ice skates!" Jaycee jumped up and down, tossing the torn wrapping paper to the side. He looked at Wesley. "Does this mean we can go skating on the pond now?"

Wesley's smile widened and he winked at Shannon. "Yes. And they're already sharpened."

"Woo hoo!" Jaycee high-fived Brighton. "I bet you got new ice skates too."

Brighton frowned. "You're not supposed to tell, Jaycee."

Jaycee looked at Holly. "And I didn't even smell them in there when we wrapped the box."

Shannon laughed. "*Smell* them?"

Holly and Randy chuckled. "It's an inside joke," Randy explained, winking at Holly.

"Can we go home right now so we can go ice skating?" Jaycee practically hollered in his enthusiasm.

"Hold up, buddy. Before we continue, Shannon and I have a surprise," Wesley said.

Randy's mom gasped.

"You guessed it." Wesley beamed. "We're expecting another little one!"

"Aww…congratulations, son!" His mother wrapped him in a hug.

"This family just keeps on growing," his dad remarked. "As it should." He congratulated Wesley and Shannon.

Randy stole a glance at Holly, his eyes sparkling.

"Don't forget, we haven't even opened Grandma and Grandpa Stoltz's present yet," his dad's enthusiastic voice practically sang the words.

"They brought us a present too?" Jaycee grinned. "*Mammi*, did you make me another scarf?"

Randy's Amish grandparents shared a smile. "Not this time."

"What is it, then?" Jaycee scratched his head.

"Patience, Jaycee," Wesley said, chuckling.

"We'll have to go outside," Grandpa Stoltz said.

"What is it? What is it?" Jaycee bounced up and down. Little Melanie mimicked her brother, although she didn't know what she was supposed to be excited about.

Holly smiled, enjoying the children. She couldn't wait for the day she'd have her own, hopefully, with Randy. He'd make a good father.

They all bundled up and headed out the door. At the same time, a truck and trailer pulled up. The trailer's contents were hidden, but the shape gave it away.

"No way!" Brighton laughed.

"Let's open it," Jaycee insisted.

Randy's father lifted the boy onto the back of the trailer after they'd loosened the bungee cords. Brighton helped to unveil their gift.

"It's *Mammi* and Santa's sleigh!" Jaycee squealed.

"This is for us?" Brighton asked.

Grandpa Stoltz nodded, looking at each of them. "*Mammi* and I are getting too old to enjoy it anymore. It's for *all* of you, but I'm guessing it'll need to be stationed at Wesley's place for now."

"Yes!" Jaycee threw his fist in the air. "Just wait until I tell the kids at school that Santa gave me his sleigh for Christmas! They're never gonna believe me."

"I'm afraid the reindeer aren't included," Grandpa Stoltz teased with a chuckle.

"Now, we get to go ice skating *and* go on a sleigh ride!" Jaycee jumped. "This is the best Christmas ever!"

And with that, Holly had to agree.

The following day, Randy and Holly joined Grandma and Grandpa Stoltz for Second Christmas.

As they sat in the toasty living room, Randy noted the clip-clop of a horse and buggy driving past. "Are you going to get into trouble because we're here?"

His grandfather shrugged. "I'm already under the *bann*. They will see that I am not following it, which I've decided I will do as *Der Herr* leads and let their actions be between them and *Gott*. I only need to give account for myself. Besides, you are our true family. We are done turning loved ones away because that is what other men want. I want to die with a clear conscience. Until recently, I've realized, I have actually been fighting *Gott* my whole life."

"What do you mean?"

"I was like the Apostle Paul before he met Jesus. I was zealous for my religion, would and did do just about anything for it. To this day, I wonder if our *kinner* would have survived the accident, had they been in an *Englisch* vehicle instead of a buggy. But I leave that in *Gott's* hands now." He wiped away regretful tears. "We had always been taught not to question the Old Ways, the ways of our Amish people. We do things because that's the way they've always been done. Like Saul, we don't stop to think that maybe we are actually going against *Gott's* will."

"Wow. I had no idea."

"But I see now that *Der Herr* is giving us a second chance. With you and Wesley. With Wesley's *kinner*, and maybe yours in the future. I *chust* want to live a life well pleasing to *Der Herr*."

Randy squeezed Holly's hand and smiled.

"And now, your *grossmudder* and I would like to give you something."

Randy's brow creased as he took the envelope from his grandfather's hand. He opened it to find a pleasant Christmas card with a wintry scene emblazoned on the front. When he lifted the top, a check slipped into his hand. He glanced down at it, then did a double take when he realized the amount. Six figures. "Grandpa, I can't take this from you."

"It is your inheritance. Well, part of it, anyhow. Wesley received his before he and Shannon were married. Your *mammi* and I thought it would be helpful in starting a home. When we pass, our property will be sold and the money will be divided between you and your brother. You are our closest living relatives and we'd like to bless you in this way."

"Wow." Randy scrubbed at his stubble, then glanced at Holly. "I don't know what to say. This is…it's… amazing. Thank you."

"You mentioned looking for a job earlier. Have you considered driving for the Amish?" His grandmother suggested.

"No, I haven't. I guess I didn't even realize that was a thing."

"Oh, it's very much 'a thing' as you say." His grandfather chuckled. "You can take some pretty nice vacations. All paid for. If you don't mind occasionally staying in Amish homes."

"Oh." He frowned. "I wouldn't want to be away from Holly. I'd be worried sick about her."

"Randy," Holly protested. "I'd be fine."

"Well, maybe save the longer trips for when you are married. Then you can both go on a vacation."

"Now, that sounds like something that might be doable." He looked at Holly, who nodded.

"But there are many Amish around here that need rides every day. To and from work. To the store. Occasionally out to dinner. Sometimes, trips into the city. And if you're ten cents cheaper than the next guy, you'll never be lacking for work."

"Hmm…well, I guess it's definitely something to ponder."

"And if *Der Herr* opens a door for you, you could share *Gott's* love with them."

"I always thought the Amish already knew God," Holly chimed in.

"Oh, they know the stories. They know *about* Jesus. But knowing about Jesus and placing your faith in Him for salvation are two different things. Don't get me wrong, some Amish *do* know Him. But sadly, just like some *Englischers*, there are many that don't have a relationship with Him. Like me, for example. I thought that if I *chust* did enough good things, if I sacrificed enough, if I suffered enough, that one day *Gott* would magically let me into His kingdom.

"But then my *sohn* showed me the verse that states *all our righteousnesses are as filthy rags*. *Gott* is not impressed with anything *I* do. *I* cannot add anything to what Jesus did when He died on the cross and rose from the dead. *He* defeated death and Hell. *I* am not a co-redeemer. *He* did the work because my work would never be *gut* enough. That was when I realized that it is Christ alone that saves. And what *Gott* desired of me was a relationship with Him."

Randy frowned. "Not to change the subject or anything, but how would I go about driving for Amish people?"

"What most do to start out is post flyers on the bulletin boards. Make those little hanging tags with your phone number on it, that people can tear off," Grandma said.

"I just put it up there and they'll call me?"

"Yep."

"Sounds like it might be a flexible option, since you'll be in school," Holly said.

Randy frowned. "About that. I've been thinking. I don't know if I want to go back."

"Randy, we've been over this before." Holly seemed put out by him. "It's your *final* semester. Just finish. Get your degree."

"I know we talked about it. But that was before I found out about your heart condition. I wanna be with you as much as possible, Holly."

"Randy..." It was the warning tone again.

"Okay. But only if you'll marry me as soon as I graduate."

Holly gasped. "Randy Travis Stoltz, are you proposing to me?"

He chuckled. "Yeah, I guess I am. Sort of."

"I don't know if I should be upset with you for not proposing properly, or if I should be excited that you're asking. Which, you haven't really asked."

"I think I'll wait to do that until I have a ring in my hand. How's that for proper?" He winked.

"That's better."

"So, is that a yes?"

Holly laughed, shaking her head. "I'll answer the question *after* you ask." Her complexion darkened. "And I think you have a pretty good idea what my answer will be."

Although they were in his Amish grandparents' home, Randy couldn't help but lean close and kiss Holly on the lips. "I think I do," he murmured.

EPILOGUE

Summer, the following year…

esley stood next to his brother, clad in a grey suit and sporting fancy cowboy boots, at the front of the church. He squeezed Randy's shoulder as he awaited his bride. Randy's smile couldn't be brighter.

The music selection changed, and the bridesmaids began their ascent up the aisle. First came Holly's sisters, then Wesley's own gorgeous wife, Shannon, stood as Holly's matron-of-honor. Next came his precious girls, four-and-a-half-year-old Melanie and two-year-old Olivia, who dropped flower petals along the aisle runner. He glanced to his wife, who evidenced the life growing within her womb, a testament to the love they shared and God's blessing upon their lives. They exchanged a smile.

Moments seemed to tick by as the doors in back of

the auditorium closed. The congregation stood as the "Wedding March" wafted through the sanctuary. The doors opened again, and his brother's bride seemed to float toward them. Wesley glanced at Randy, who clenched and unclenched his hands.

Randy wiped away a tear, but his smile never dimmed. "She's so beautiful." His brother couldn't seem to take his eyes off his bride-to-be as he walked down the steps of the platform to claim Holly from her father's arm.

Wesley looked out at the wedding guests. Among them were Holly's parents and extended family, members of their church congregation, his and Randy's parents, and both sets of grandparents, including Grandpa and Grandma Stoltz, dressed in Amish attire.

His paternal grandparents had been excommunicated from their Amish fellowship, but still held onto the core values of their community. Now they could openly fellowship with their entire family, which fulfilled a lifelong desire in their hearts. Wesley realized that sometimes one had to lose something valuable to gain something greater, but doing so required faith in the God who fashioned each of them.

When the preacher announced Randy and Holly as husband and wife, his brother probably broke the record for the longest wedding kiss in the history of the church. This resulted in the hooting and hollering of the wedding party, who shared smiles all around.

God knew all along that Holly was the perfect match for Randy. She had not only encouraged him in his relationship with God, but she'd taught him how to love with his whole heart. And Wesley had no doubt that the two of them would live happily ever after, by God's grace.

THE END

Thanks for reading!

Word of mouth is one of the best forms of advertisement and a HUGE blessing to the author. If you enjoyed this book, **please** consider leaving a review, sharing on social media, and telling your reading friends.

THANK YOU!

DISCUSSION QUESTIONS

1. What was your first impression of Randy Stoltz? Did it change by the end of the book?

2. When the event in the ice skating rink occurred, did you think Randy's behavior was inappropriate? Why?

3. Once Randy decided Lisa wasn't 'the one,' do you think he was right to end things with her, or do you think he should have waited longer? Have you ever been a participant in a one-sided relationship?

4. Randy and Holly are virtual opposites. Do you believe that opposites attract? Have you ever been in a relationship with someone who is opposite of you? Are/were there ways you are/were alike?

5. Have you ever heard of courting the way Holly's family practiced it? What are your thoughts on courting verses dating?

6. Randy and his brother, Wesley, get along well. How many siblings do you have? Do you get along with them?

7. When Holly discovered Randy's aversion to his Amish grandparents, she desired to help him resolve his issues. Are there rifts in any relationship in your life that need mending? How can you take steps toward that goal?

8. When it comes to Holly's heart, Randy's charming ways are quite persuasive. Have you ever been persuaded to do things you know you shouldn't do?

9. Holly's influence in Randy's life compels him to learn more about the things of God. Do you have someone in your life that influences you for good?

10. Christopher is grieved when he realizes it was his own actions that repelled his grandson, but it opens his eyes to something even greater—what real love looks like. Have you ever thought you were doing something right, then learned it was actually wrong?

11. Although Christopher and Judy lost something important to them, they found something equally precious. Have you ever had to lose something in order to gain something else?

12. Holly's revelation rocked Randy's world? If you've experienced something similar, how did you cope?

13. Have you ever been Christmas caroling? What is your favorite Christmas song?

14. Do you enjoy the holiday season? What is your favorite part?

15. If you enjoyed this story, will you kindly consider leaving a review? Thanks

A SPECIAL THANK YOU

I'd like to take this time to thank everyone that had any involvement in this book and its production, including my Mom and Dad, who have always been supportive of my writing, my longsuffering Family—especially my handsome, encouraging Hubby, my Amish and former-Amish friends who have helped immensely in my understanding of the Amish ways, my supportive Pastor and Church family, my Proofreaders, my Editor, my CIA Facebook author friends who have been a tremendous help, my wonderful Readers who buy, read, offer great input, and leave encouraging reviews and emails, my awesome Launch Team who, I'm confident, will 'Sprede the Word' about *Unlikely Sweethearts*! And last, but certainly not least, I'd like to thank my ***Precious LORD and SAVIOUR JESUS CHRIST***, for without Him, none of this would have been possible!

Made in the USA
Coppell, TX
18 March 2021

51883470R00152